DARK & DECEITFUL

BINK CUMMINGS

Dark & Deceitful

Discrete Edition

Contact the Author:
Email: BinkCummings@yahoo.com

Editor: Mary Sittu-Kern
Cover Model: Alex Turner
Photographer: Golden Czermak
Cover Designer: Bink Cummings
Beta Readers: Holly, Sandie, Jayne, Janell

To my badass sisters who've risen from the ashes of every battle they've fought. May you always find the strength to be unapologetically yourself - today, tomorrow, and always.

AUTHOR NOTE

Dear Sacred Sister,

This page is for those who need access to possible reading triggers. If you have none, please skip this page.

This book contains the following elements in varying degrees.

Mild Cheating

Assault

Graphic Violence

Graphic Spicy Scenes

Trafficking

ONE

Humming to myself, I select my favorite loose-leaf tea from the lineup of vintage floral tins on my kitchen counter and fill my infuser—a mini teapot with holes. Draping its chain over the edge of my favorite hand-thrown mug, I set it aside to open a tin of homemade hot chocolate mix with mini marshmallows—a special blend I made myself. Heap after heap of chocolate dust fills the bottom of a pink polka-dotted mug until I'm satisfied with its yum factor. That's a must. Nobody likes a cheap, flavorless hot chocolate—wouldn't you agree?

From the stovetop, steam rises from my pot of milk just as my kettle of water informs me it's ready. Wasting little time, I add milk to the hot cocoa. Using anything but milk is blasphemous. The hot water from my electric kettle goes into my mug to steep the orange chamomile tea. A quick mix, mix, mix with a spoon in the hot chocolate, and it's ready just as the suction releasing my front door rattles the blinds, and the familiar sound of boot heels scrapes across my mahogany floor.

The television clicks on, filling a once peaceful house with noise.

Hairs on the back of my neck stand on end, sending a ripple down my spine as I feel him before I see him.

It's always been this way.

A sense of knowing.

A strange tether. A connection.

I hate it almost as much as I hate him.

His familiar scent fills the kitchen—rich, woodsy, expensive, mixed with a pinch of lavender and bergamot.

Forcing a smile for both our sakes, I turn to find a muscular shoulder propped against my kitchen wall and arms tucked loosely across a broad chest. He dressed up tonight—black jeans, a navy button-up with a crisp collar, undone at the top, exposing not only his thick neck but his intricate, black-and-gray skull with roses tattoo. It wraps around the front of his throat and ends at the sharp cut of his jawline. His shirt sleeves are folded neatly just below the elbow, showing off his impressive, inked forearms. A stack of leather bracelets adorns one wrist. A black watch decorates the other.

My perusal is quick and detached—nothing more than an appreciation of the human form standing in my home. Before my unwelcome guest gets any ideas, like the desire to chat, I return to my task at hand and busy myself in the kitchen.

In the microwave, I toss in a bag of popcorn and hit the necessary button. Then I scrub the counters I scrubbed an hour ago, ya know, to avoid looking at him, speaking, or pretty much anything else.

"You have another stalker," he announces.

I heave an internal sigh.

Not this shit again.

I have a lot of things—tattoos, brown hair, and a love of plants, to name a few. Sure, a stalker could be added to that list. They happen without fail time and time again. Most people have a *thing*. Some are clumsy, so they trip and fall more than the average person. Others might lose their keys all the time or misplace their phone. I collect stalkers like a prostitute collects STIs. It's my *thing*...or one of them.

When I don't respond, Captain Obvious chuckles as if he finds this amusing—finds me amusing.

Trust me, if I had it in my heart to kill him so I could avoid these painful interactions, I would have done it years ago. Unfortunately, I'm too nice.

As the popcorn does its thing, I toss my rag in the sink and cross both arms over my chest to keep from fidgeting. Standing at the tall kitchen window facing the street, I watch his woman pace up and down the sidewalk beneath the faint glow of the streetlights, waiting for him to leave because she refuses to come inside, despite years of endless invitations.

Month after month, this awful cycle persists. The seasons may come and go, but this endures like a cancer, eating away at everything and everyone... well, me.

On the opposite side of the road in our sleepy little suburb sits a blue sedan and, in the driver's seat, my latest stalker, watching me. Sure, I can't see his eyes, but his body's angled this way. The man either doesn't care I can see him, or he thinks the night somehow shields the obvious. I'd guess the former, given how long he's been parked there—on and off the past week. At first, I thought he was visiting a neighbor. The holiday season is fast approaching, so that wouldn't be out of the question. Though, we don't have many neighbors. My street was the last built in this community and abuts a protected forest and commercially owned farmland. There are no houses across from me and only three down the way. That's why I moved here—the peace and quiet. That's also why any car out-of-place sticks out like a sore thumb.

Oh, I know. I'm sure you hear the word stalker and freak the hell out. You'd call the cops and file a restraining order. I'd tell you to do the same unless you lived in my world. Trust me, nothing scares me, least of all the man in the blue sedan.

"Earth to Kali." My visitor's footsteps grow closer.

My heart ratches up into my throat, emotions clogging there like a stopper in a drain.

Alright, so perhaps there's one thing that scares me—him.

A hand touches my shoulder in a simple gesture, but I feel it everywhere—a lance through my heart, the penetrating heat through the cotton of my pajamas, the… Fuck this… Shrugging off his touch, I shuffle to the other side of the kitchen. With the island between us, I draw in a lungful of air. Hold. Release. Only then do I set my palms on the cool granite and stare him down… because this has to stop. He shouldn't be here.

"Leave, Dark." The weight of my words echoes through the space.

Across the island, he looks down at me with a softness that could only be read as pity… remorse. Something. "You know I can't do that."

"Yes. You can. We do this every fucking month. Sometimes more than that. You don't have to come inside. We don't have to talk."

"You're my wife."

And there it is.

The same bullshit… a different day.

He's right, though.

I am his wife. We've been married for over twenty years and have two grown sons together.

There's a lifetime of memories between us.

And a lifetime of deceit.

Shaking my head in disgust, I scoot the mugs to the edge of the counter and give them both a final stir before I remove the spoons and the infuser and set them in the sink to wash later. Retrieving the popcorn from the microwave, I dump it into a bowl from the cupboard and set it next to our drinks.

"Lily," I call to my adorable, dark-haired, gray-eyed visitor, who looks exactly like her father. "Come get your hot chocolate and popcorn."

Lily skips in from the living room in her fluffy slipper socks and takes one look at her dad, who blows her a kiss. She catches it with a giggle and smacks it to her cheek before snatching up her goodies and carrying them into the living room for our girls' night.

"Thanks, Kali!" she hollers around a mouthful of popcorn.

"Pick a movie. I'll be there in a bit," I respond with a fond smile, knowing exactly what she'll choose. It's tradition. You know how kids are. They get an idea in their head, and it turns to cement. I've watched the same movie every month for the past eighteen months. Not that I mind. We recite certain spots, word for word, and made it a game to see who can do it the most. I'll tell you a secret—I let her win.

The telltale sound of *Coraline* beginning is my cue to get Dark the hell out of my house and on the date with his woman. This is Lily's and my time together.

Knowing the only way to get Dark to leave, I return to my spot on the side of the island and pull open the drawer with the hidden compartment. Dark's eyes widen when he realizes what I'm doing. I extract one of the many guns hidden throughout my home, set it on the counter, and make a show of unlocking the safety. You don't marry a Sacred Sinner nomad without knowing how to protect yourself.

"Leave," I growl, staring daggers at him.

The asshole grins and out pops those stupid dimples. "You and I both know you won't use that on me."

"Do we?" Because I'm not so sure.

"Kali," he placates, like I'm a child who needs a pat on the head.

"I asked you to leave."

"Why are you so fuckin' pissed at me today?"

"You know why," I growl.

Most days, I'm civil to Dark. I can be the bigger person. Put on a smile. Endure. Today is not that day… and if he's asking why I'm pissed, why I'm edgy, why I want to rip his too-attractive throat out, then he's already forgotten. Not that that surprises me. It's been years. One never forgets the eve of the anniversary of the day your husband returned from a club run with a new woman and a newborn baby. For eighteen months, he disappeared—fourteen months longer than we had planned. Nobody knew where he was. Nobody could find him. Not even his father.

Eight years tomorrow, he showed up on this very doorstep with that little girl sitting in my living room. He begged to explain what happened and asked for forgiveness he doesn't deserve. That same week, he bought the house two down from mine, making us neighbors. A month later, he and his new family moved into that house… and he's been here ever since.

After nearly a decade, you'd think I'd let it go.

I haven't.

Can't.

Dark stares at me with his impossibly gray eyes, deep in thought. I know that look well—the wrinkle between his brows, the purse of his full lips.

When nothing registers in that brain of his, I die a little more.

Another crack forms in my already broken heart.

I swallow hard to keep myself in check, refusing to show weakness.

I will not cry.

Not now.

Not in front of him.

Not when Lily is waiting for me to watch *Coraline,* in our matching pajamas—black-with-white skulls. It's our thing. She may not be mine. She may be the byproduct of her father's infidelity. But from the first moment I saw her on that stoop, wrapped in her ladybug blanket, I loved her as if she were my own. Alright, maybe not right away. There was shock and tears involved. After that, when things died down, and I adjusted to my new normal, we bonded—hard.

Not giving Dark time to draw his own conclusion and refusing to admit it still bothers me, I return the gun to the drawer, snatch my tea, and find Lily in the living room, snuggled up on my black, overstuffed couch. I set my mug on the end table and drop beside her. Lily drapes our favorite raven blanket across our laps and presses play to start girls' night.

And just like that… Dark's forgotten.

Poof.

A distant memory.

At least for a little while.

Whenever he finally leaves to go on his date with Abby, I don't hear him go.

Lily's word-for-word reciting of *Coraline* makes enduring her father worth it.

For hours, it's us girls and our movies.

After our third show, well past Lily's bedtime, we clean up our mess in the living room before we finish with our nightly ritual.

Petting a raven's head that's perched on a wooden branch on the console table by the front door, Lily whispers a secret into his ear and removes the smudge stick from his mouth. I extract the matches from the drawer in the end table as Lily approaches with the new stick I made with desert sage and lavender—to clean, bless, heal, remove negativity, and promote calmness.

I'm teaching her the ways—of new and old.

Just as my mother did.

Where my sons have followed in their father's footsteps—Lily's early fascination with what Mother Nature offers has been an unexpected but welcome blessing.

Together, we light the smudge stick by the front door and walk through my home, turning clockwise within each room and opening a window to let all the negative energy out. We offer the universe our quiet chants, in various tongues, my mother taught me.

At the back door, Lily retrieves the bowl of sand to extinguish the sage and lavender stick.

Now it's time for rest.

Up the stairs, I follow her to her eldest brother's bedroom—Tarek's. He moved out years ago. Now a patched Sacred Sinner living across the country, I don't see him much, but we talk or text often. Lily has turned his old room into her own when she stays the night.

The adorable girl crawls into the bed as I retrieve the chamomile and lavender oil from the nightstand. Sitting on the edge of the mattress beside her, I tuck Lily in as she snuggles down into the pillows and puts her arms out, palms up.

I open the bottle and apply a single droplet to the inside of her wrists. She rubs them together before audibly inhaling the scent and sighing. "I love this stuff," she notes. Smiling wide, Lily shows off her pearly whites—one crooked, another just starting to come in.

"Do you still have the bottle at home?" Lily loves essential oils, so I've made sure she has whatever scents on hand to use, even when I'm not around.

"Yes." She wiggles around under the blanket, getting comfy.

"Does Dad put it on you each night?"

"If I ask him to."

Satisfied with her answer, I lean in and kiss her forehead. "Love you, kiddo. Thanks for another fun girls' night."

Little arms circle my neck in a brief hug. "Love you, too." She squeezes once and frees me. It reminds me of the days when my boys were little—our nightly rituals were much like this. We lived in a much smaller home back then—a two-bedroom, single-story 1950s-era rental with their father. That was long ago. Nine years, to be exact. When Dark never returned home, and our year lease was up, I needed to get out. Living there when I didn't know if my husband was dead or alive, with all those memories held within those walls, wasn't healthy for me. So, I got my first mortgage with the help of another and started anew in more ways than one. It's crazy to think I'll have met this little girl eight years ago tomorrow.

A final blanket tuck around Lily, and her eyes drift closed.

Off the lights go as I depart, leaving my favorite eight-year-old to get a good night's rest. Tomorrow morning, she'll run home after breakfast, and I'll handle this stalker situation.

Ugh.

Stalkers.

They're the worst.

TWO

Mmmmm. Bacon. Bacon. Bacon and sweet mapley syrup.

I crack open an eye as the tastiest of tasty aromas weave through the house. Not that it has far to travel with my bedroom on the first floor, close to the kitchen. Someone's here, and they're cooking, that much I know.

Stretching my arms over my head, I knock both hands into my black padded headboard as a tired smile breaks the surface, along with a groan. Today might be the day that shall not be named... but who am I to complain if it's starting like this?

Knowing it can only be one of four people inviting themselves here without giving me a heads-up, I don't bother getting dressed when I climb out of bed and fold the covers back down because I'm proper like that. I slip on my favorite black moccasin slippers and pad my way out of the bedroom and into the main part of the house, where the scent intensifies, and my tummy groans in hunger.

Water runs in the sink, and a ceramic bowl clinks as I enter the kitchen and get an eyeful of a bare tattooed back, gray hair, and dark jeans riding low on a tapered waist. Not wanting to disturb my visitor, I smile so damn big my cheeks hurt as I watch him work his magic on the stove, humming to himself.

I can't believe he remembered.

Of course he did.

He remembers everything.

The man dances around the space as if it's second nature to him as I remove a plant from a small table in the corner and prop the edge of my butt on it to watch him work.

"Kali, you can say hello. I promise I don't bite," the sneaky man announces as he continues to cook whatever's in the pan on the stove.

Busted.

"I didn't want to disturb you." More like I want to watch him cook me food because men don't cook for me. Well, none of them except this one.

Wiping his hands on a towel, my visitor pats his hip as if I'm supposed to join him. Hopping down from my spot, I put the plant back where it belongs and do just that.

Dropping everything he's doing to greet me, Sunshine swoops me into his arms. My stomach rolls in wild somersaults as he plops me on the kitchen island and inserts himself between my parted thighs. I gasp as the cold granite freezes my barely covered behind, and he laughs. Then he does what Sunshine always does—gives me a full once-over, checking to make sure I'm okay. I'm not sure why he does it, but he's done it for as long as I've known him.

A pair of big hands rub up and down my bare arms as his concerned gaze delves into mine. "You whole?" A graying eyebrow hikes in question.

I nod. "Yes." Of course, I'm whole. I'm breathing.

Nothing is truly broken. My life, for all intents and purposes, is spectacular, barring the stalker issues and the anniversary of… ya know. You've just caught me at a bad time. I promise it's not normally like this.

"Even today?" Those same hands pause at my waist and give it a squeeze.

"Yes. Is that why you're here?" I ask. I told you he wouldn't forget.

"Yes and no." He hems and haws. "I have a couple'a gifts for you."

"Gift *gifts* or gifts?" Either is fine. But gift gifts are extra special. They're the best. They're my favorite.

"Gift gifts." He winks, oozing hot-man energy.

Mashing my lips together so I don't let out a girlish squeal, my eyes round in delight.

Sunshine chuckles warmly, drawing circles at my hips.

"Where?" I ask, rubbing my heel along the backside of his thigh.

"At the store. I wanted to feed ya first." He gestures toward the stove and the plates he already set out.

Of course, he did—this man. I don't know what I ever did to deserve him.

I glance over my shoulder to see if the little lady's up yet. "Where's Lily?"

"I fed her a bowl of cereal after my shower, and then I sent her home."

He sent her home… but…

Confused by the turn of events, wrinkles bunch on my forehead and nose. "You showered upstairs?"

"Yeah. Because I didn't wanna wake you."

Looking him in the eye, I drop my hands on his shoulders. His skin's hot and smooth to the touch. "You know I don't mind." There's an entire caddy of his bathroom essentials under my sink. My bathroom is perfection. An oasis. He loves relaxing there after long weeks on the road.

"But *I* do," he replies. "Lily said you watched three movies last night and voo-doo-hoo-doo'd the house. You needed the sleep."

I chuckle at his choice of words. There's nothing voodoo about smudging. "I always cleanse the house."

Sunshine smirks, and his head tilts to the side knowingly. "Yeah. When Dark's over." He cocks his brow in question, daring me to argue.

He's right.

I do it to get rid of Dark's bad juju. Who can blame me?

As if summoned by the Devil himself, my front door opens, the blinds rattle, and thunderous footfalls echo through my house. Sighing at what's about to go down, I peek over my shoulder to find the bane of my existence standing right where he was yesterday, this time in a pair of gray sweats, a blue, long-sleeved shirt pushed up his forearms, and a glower—an ugly one.

Not wanting to see him today of all days, I pretend Dark's not here and bury my face in the side of Sunshine's neck. It smells of manly soap and all things safe and yummy. Knowing damn well this won't go over well, the man between my legs wraps both of his arms around me in protection from the big bad biker coming to start shit. It takes one to know one, and Dark knows he's no match for Sunshine. But that won't stop what's about to ensue. Two bulls in the same room never end well.

"What the fuck are you doing here?!" Dark roars at Sunshine when neither one of us addresses his existence. "My daughter comes home, and I look outside to not only find the stalker gone but also your fuckin' van in Kali's driveway. Aren't you supposed to be out on assignment?"

"This is my assignment," Sunshine replies, as smooth as butter.

"Bullshit."

"It is. I got here at four this mornin' and had time to spare, so I took care of the stalker. Why the hell do you care?"

Dark growls.

Sunshine snorts, not the least bit amused by Dark's interruption. "That's what I thought. Now go the fuck home and leave us to have a peaceful breakfast."

Yes. What he said. That sounds perfect. You tell him, Sunshine.

"You know I'm not gonna do that." A typical Dark response.

"Why not? Are you here to rub salt in wounds?" Firm palms run up and down my spine in reassurance as I squeeze my eyes shut in hopes Dark gets a clue and leaves of his own volition.

Another one of those angry growls surfaces. "What the hell are you yappin' about?"

"Christ." I can practically hear Sunshine's eyes roll. "Look at a calendar, will ya? Do some soul-searching. Maybe stop being a selfish prick for once in your goddamn life."

There's shuffling, followed by a lovely paragraph or two of angry expletives courtesy of Dark. Suddenly, I'm no longer hungry, and I just want to go back to sleep for a year, maybe two—no more yummy bacon and syrup for this lady.

"Kali." My name on Dark's lips, soft and broken, aches in places I don't wish to acknowledge.

Stiffening against me, Sunshine's chest vibrates in a low, scary timbre. "Go. Home. Dark."

"Fuck you, Pops. You know I can't do that."

Sunshine's hand cuffs around the base of my neck. "Go. Home. Dark. I won't tell you again."

"Kali." Dark's voice cracks, forcing me to swallow hard. My shoulders slump forward. I will not feel sorry for him. I won't absolve him of his fuckups. Year after year, he begs for forgiveness. The weight of his guilt he wants me to bear, and I don't know why.

Knowing me better than anyone, Sunshine taps the side of my bare legs. I lock my ankles around his waist. Supportive hands scoop under my ass cheeks and lift me from the counter. Across the house, my favorite person in the entire world carries me away from my problems and into the solace of my room. He sets me on my side of the bed, props my back against the headboard, pecks my temple, and covers my legs with all the blankets. Without a word, Sunshine turns on music from his phone, sets it on the nightstand, and leaves to take care of his son. Because that's how this always goes. Sunshine visits me and his grandbabies, and Dark loses his shit. They have an intense love-hate relationship. It wasn't always this way. Sure, they used to butt heads like any father and son would. This started after Dark returned to find Sunshine helped me buy this house. He paid the down payment, co-signed for it, and made sure the deed was in my name and my name alone—so Dark had no way of touching it and ripping my life out from under me like he'd done once before.

Sunshine has always been a constant.

A pillar of strength.

Sure, he lives on the road—a nomad to the core.

But this home is his home. We're his base—his family.

Even before Abby and Lily came along, when we lived in the rental, he stayed with us whenever he could.

Dark never minded then.

He minds now.

He minds a lot.

Closing my eyes, I release the world's longest sigh as their fighting ensues—the volume of Metallica be damned.

"You don't get to swoop in and be her knight in shining fucking armor!" Dark roars beyond my closed bedroom door.

"Leave. Before you can't take back whatever dumb shit you're about to say," Sunshine volleys in return.

"You aren't supposed to be here."

"This is my home."

"No. It's not. This is Kali's home."

"Then why do I have a house key and you don't?" Sunshine growls, and I can't help but smile at the truth of that. No matter how hard Dark has tried over the years, I've never given him a key. Each of my sons has one, as well as a few of my friends and, of course, Sunshine.

"She is *my* wife," Dark argues lamely, like that somehow matters.

"Ex-wife, or did you forget you have an entire fuckin' family two houses down, son? The name Abby ring any bells?"

"Fuck you."

"No. Fuck you for comin' over here, swingin' your dick, thinkin' it was gonna change things."

Silence.

Sunshine doesn't relent. "You spend a lot of time tryin' to piss her off and meddle in our friendship. Time you should be spendin' doin' other shit, like, oh, I dunno, quit pushin' her buttons and give her the space she's asked for. Especially today. You went out last night with your woman, and she watched your kid, then you storm over here when you saw my van? You're a whole-ass adult. Fuckin' act like one."

"I didn't realize what today was," Dark returns, sounding like a wounded toddler.

"And whose fault is that? Not mine and sure as hell not hers."

Fact is, I don't need Sunshine to fight my battles. I'm more than capable of doing it myself. But I'm tired. Too tired to deal with this today of all days. Him showing up to be here for me, to make me breakfast, and deal with another fallout with Dark, shouldn't please me as much as it does, but I'm relieved.

"I was gonna handle the stalker," Dark replies, and I snort.

"Kali doesn't need your help, Dark."

That's my cue to zone out. No. It's my cue to shower. I don't need to hear any more after this. Tearing the blankets off my legs, I beeline to my bathroom and turn on the water to drown out their escalating fight. This is normal anytime Sunshine's in town. They fight. They make up. Life moves on. Repeat.

Getting down to business, I toss my boy-short panties and tank into the hamper and go about washing up. The heat relaxes my muscles, and the lavender soap soothes my soul. Taking my time, I lather my brown hair and condition it twice to take my time. Shaving is the last hurrah. Not that I like to shave. Does any woman? I was raised by a mother who preferred to be au natural. Can't say I picked that up. A smooth pussy, legs, and armpits does a lady good. At least, this lady. You do whatever works for you. No shame.

Sufficiently clean and smooth, I turn off the water and open my glass shower door coated in steam. The noises from before have disappeared. I breathe a sigh of relief, knowing Dark is likely gone, which means special time with Sunshine—also bacon. Because yum.

Out of a heated bin, I claim a fluffy black towel, wrap it around my wet self, and trail droplets of water across the tiled bathroom floor and into the bedroom. There, I find a shirtless, gray-haired, bearded man sitting on my bed with a wooden tray laden with juice and food. The same tray I used to serve my children breakfast in bed on their birthdays when they were little.

Sunshine pats the spot next to him—my side of the mattress.

Not caring if I look like a drowned rat, I tuck my towel tighter around my chest and don't bother getting dressed before eating because that stack of French toast has my mouth watering.

"Sorry about that." Sunshine squeezes my leg as I sit down, then covers me again with the blankets, careful not to topple the tray.

I snatch a slice of bacon, lean back against the head-board, close my eyes, and bite. The pleasured sigh that rises would be embarrassing if I were in any other company. With Sunshine, I don't worry about a thing. Not once has this man ever judged me. For that, I'm grateful.

Taking my time, I chew and swallow through the entire slice, savoring the salty pork, savoring the moment, centering myself. Doing as my mother taught me, I fall into a state of peace, no longer bogged down by Dark's presence. This is my home. My bed. I'm free. I'm happy. I'm me.

Giving me all the time in the world to adjust, Sunshine waits for my eyes to open, and when they do, he's right there, my pillar, eating his bacon, wearing the kindest of eye-crinkling smiles. "Hey there, Sweets."

A soft, relieved smile surfaces. "Hi, Colton. I know I didn't have time to say it, but I missed you."

Blowing out a breath as if he needed to hear those words after the fight with his son, Sunshine draws the tray up the bed, closer for us to reach. "I missed you, too. Now let's get you fed, so I take you to your gifts. Yeah?" He sets my fork on my plate and drizzles syrup over the slices of French toast he made just for me.

On a nod, I grab my food and set it on my lap, not caring the slightest that I'm naked from the waist down under the covers or that my ex's father is eating in bed with me. This isn't a first, nor will it be a last.

"Do you remember the first time you made me French toast and bacon?" I ask as I cut a hardy piece with the side of my fork.

"It was the morning we had your mother's celebration of life."

It was.

"We'd only met, what? A few weeks before?" I draw from memory. It was so long ago.

"Yes, and you've been ours ever since."

A calm, all-encompassing warmth flows through me from the top of my head down to the tips of my black-painted toes at Sunshine's words. I *have* been theirs ever since.

THREE

Past

Age 16

HOLDING my mother's frail hand, covered with bruises from all her IV pokes, I commit every breath she takes, every soft smile and moment with her to memory, and wrap it up with a bow to carry for the rest of my life. Every second is a gift I refuse to squander. We don't have much time left. She's already lived longer than we expected.

She's my person.

My only person.

Once she's gone, I don't know what I'll do. We never thought that far. Our house is gone–foreclosed on months after she got sick. We hadn't even owned it for a year. It's a blessing we could even get her in here—the hospice wing of a nursing home, hours from where we last called home. During the day, I'm here with her through the good and the bad. At night, I sleep in our van in the parking lot outside.

The nurses know what I'm doing, and thankfully, they haven't called CPS. Not yet anyhow.

We have a week left, maybe two. Stage four pancreatic cancer is a sneaky bastard. The yellowing of Mom's skin, the frailty, the brittle nails and hair, and the pain, it's the worst. She sleeps almost all the time now.

"Kali." Mom's voice cracks with exhaustion as her hand squeezes mine with what little strength she has left, and her eyes remain shut.

"I'm here, Mom." I scoot closer to the bed, should she open her eyes today and want to see me. That happens less and less now—a minute or two here and there.

"Did I ever tell you of the time I had a foursome in a tent at a peace rally?" she rasps barely above a whisper.

Chuckling, I shake my head at the story she most definitely told me when I was far too young to understand what a foursome meant. "Yes, Mom. You did."

She releases her own version of laughter. It's weak, but I'll take anything I can get. "You should try it."

I snort as a lopsided smile briefly transforms my face into something other than worry. "I'll take that under advisement." Or I won't. Because I've never had a boyfriend, let alone the desire to share multiple men. I wouldn't know the first thing to do with one penis, let alone multiple. Bleck.

She goes on. "One of the men could have been your father."

"I know." That's how all of Mom's stories go—sharing far too much information about her sexual freedoms and finishing it with how one of those men could have been my father. A free spirit to the core, Mom has never lived by social norms. I've been homeschooled all my life, never to make any real friends apart from those we met on our many adventures. Since the day I was born in the bathroom stall at a rock concert, I think it was Bon Jovi, or was it Kiss? I can't remember. It's been us against the world. Or that's what Mom has always said.

"Do you think there will be peace when I die?" she whispers to herself or one of the many invisible friends she's made as of late. They talk for hours sometimes. The spirits, she calls them. We don't believe in Christianity or God. Not in the traditional, holy, worship-me-or-you'll-go-to-Hell sense. Mom's a scholar of the world, and she's taught me much about worldly religions, new and old. When she dies, finishing her pilgrimage of life, my hope is she's reborn again —following the cycle of samsara.

Leaving her to talk to her visitors in private, I carefully set Mom's hand back on the edge of the bed, on top of her crocheted blanket. Not knowing if she'll be alive when I return, I peck her forehead, and she hums as if she knows I'm there.

"I love you. You can go whenever you're ready."

Mom hums once more as I depart and turns her head slightly to whisper to her spirits once more, this time in Gaelic, a language she picked up from her time in Scotland, years before I was born.

Outside her room, I stop to breathe as a young, blonde nurse I see every day walks by to check on us. "How are you, Kali?"

"As good as I can be. She's busy." I nod toward Mom's closed door.

"Talking to the Viking?"

I shrug. "No? Maybe?"

Nurse Christy smiles warmly and pats me on the shoulder. "If you need anything, you know where to find me."

"Thanks."

In the hospice wing, I make my way to the small kitchen and sitting room they have for visiting family—something plucked right out of the nineteen-eighties with its paneled walls, brown carpet, and ugly couches. If I'm not with my mom, I'm here, taking a break and eating whatever they have in stock because I have no money for food, gas, or… well, anything. The nurses have been kind enough to leave extras for me—a hot meal here, an extra sandwich there. Each is left with a sticky note and my name on it. It's pity food for the girl with the dying mom, but beggars can't be choosers.

Peeling the purple note from a sub in the fridge, I unwrap the foot-long and carry it, along with a bottle of water, over to the couch to eat. The television is on in the corner, playing the Soaps with closed captioning to keep the volume down.

Margaret and Deacon sure hate each other in today's episode.

A door opens and closes. There's a masculine clearing of a throat.

I freeze at the sound and crane my neck to see who's here. A man with dark hair, the most startling gray eyes, and the kindest smile lifts his chin at me just inside the door. I forget to blink, much less say hello. I simply stare, wide-eyed and dumbstruck, because *holy hotness*. He's wearing a vest. It's black leather with patches all over.

His smile widens, showing off a row of pearly whites as his head tilts to the side, watching me watch him, as if he doesn't have a single care in the world. That makes one of us. Lucky guy.

The door behind him opens, and my mouth falls open as

a boy, no, *man*, much closer to my age than the other, steps around the other gentleman—same hair color, same eyes, same height, similar build. Oh, wow… there are two of them. Father and son?

The newcomer doesn't notice my awe because he doesn't even notice me as he addresses his brother… Friend?

"Pops, why you standin' here?"

Ah.

His father.

Makes sense.

Pops, the man in question, tilts his chin at me, and that's when the spell breaks, and I jerk around, face-forward, cheeks blazing as hot as the sun. Hunching forward to look as small as humanly possible, I take enormous bites of my sub to get it eaten before they get a chance to talk to me. Because what would I say? What do you say to those visiting the hospice wing? The only other people I've encountered in this room were two elderly women saying goodbye to their husbands, and they sobbed. We didn't talk.

The opposite side of the couch dips, and a wave of nerves crashes through me.

"I'm Sunshine," the older man introduces.

I say nothing and stuff more of the sub into my mouth.

What kind of name is Sunshine?

Odd.

Out of the corner of my eye, I notice Sunshine leaning back on the sofa. A booted foot props on his holey, jean-clad knee as he relaxes into the cushions and drapes an arm across the back like a cool guy in the movies.

"I'm Dark," the other male says from somewhere else in the room. I'm too chicken shit to look up and find out.

Acutely aware of their presence, I fidget as I swallow and

dive in for a bite so big my cheeks burst like a chipmunk. Sweat dots my brow, and I let out a small squeak when I choke on the dry, flavorless bread. Not wanting to die in front of these men, I spit part of my sub onto the wrapper in my lap and cringe at the half-chewed bits. I cover them quickly with my hand.

The younger male chuckles as I tremble.

I need to go.

I need to check on my mother.

Time to get up and walk away. Stand proud. Pretend to be cool.

Pretend. To. Be. Cool.

"Hey." A hand touches my shoulder. I jerk so hard in surprise that my food, the chewed-up bits and all, along with my water bottle, tumble to the floor at my feet.

I drop to my knees on the ugly carpet and scramble to pick up the mess.

Stupid.

So stupid.

The man from the couch kneels beside me. "Hey. Hey. It's okay."

No.

No, it's not okay.

My mom is dying.

I'm without a home.

Without food or money.

I haven't graduated from high school yet.

I have weeks until she's gone.

Weeks until I am alone.

Fat tears pour down my cheeks—hot, traitorous, horribly embarrassing tears. Tears I can't stop.

The man… Sunshine, yeah, that's his name, doesn't seem

to care when he scoops up my mess into his hand as I sit on my knees, chin on my chest, and crumble like a deck of cards.

A hiccupped cry rips from my throat at his unexpected kindness. At everything.

Then suddenly, he's just there.

His warmth.

His presence.

Scooping me off the floor, Sunshine sits on the couch with me on his lap. To hide myself from him and the world, I stuff my face into the side of his throat and paint it in salty anguish.

"Shhhh. It's okay. It's okay," he soothes, rubbing a hand up and down the side of my thigh.

There's a throat clearing, and someone stuffs a wad of tissues into my hand. I clutch them to my chest like a lifeline.

"I'm so sorry," I blubber against the stranger's neck.

"It's gonna be okay, sweetheart." He rocks me against him and hums. The scent of aftershave and leather mixed with his soothing sounds somehow calms me a little, just enough to breathe deep and stop shaking.

I'll never be okay again.

Not after this.

My mom is dying.

And she's all I got.

FOUR

Present Day

STANDING in front of the bathroom mirror, I smooth a hand down the side of my floor-length, patchwork, earth-toned boho skirt. It's wrinkly. It's supposed to be. It adds texture, but I don't know if this is the right outfit to wear to the shop today… ya know, on *the* day. Perhaps I should rock head-to-toe black. Meh. I don't know why I'm overthinking this.

Grumbling at my indecision, I adjust my knitted, copper-colored, cropped tank so my bra doesn't show. I picked this little cutie up from a boutique in the town over. It's hand-made perfection. There's something special about wearing clothes made by another person, not a machine. Don't you agree?

On one of the talon jewelry hooks on my wall, I untangle my cream macramé necklace and dig through my crystal-filled selenite bowl in the corner of my vanity. Did you know selenite cleanses crystals? If you didn't. Now you do. I select a gorgeous, tumbled tiger's eye because it matches my outfit and provides protection. Slipping the wooden bead up the necklace, I place the crystal inside, slide the bead back into place, and over my head it goes, setting in the space between my breasts. To connect with Mother Earth in one of the many ways my mother taught me, I pick two much smaller tumbled crystals from the bowl and tuck them into my bra, underneath my breasts, so you can't see the slight bulge. Boob rocks are what I've grown to call them. Silly, perhaps. But I would rather go into the world protected in any way possible—a little jade for luck and carnelian for courage doesn't hurt anyone.

Sorting through more necklaces, and I have a ton, I pick two more in varying lengths to layer. From another hook, I collect a shitload of bracelets—some beaded, some braided, and a few jangly ones, all of them in tones that compliment my outfit.

If you haven't caught on yet, I'm stalling.

Sunshine's in the living room, doom scrolling on his phone as I drag my feet. Sure, I'm excited to see whatever gift gifts he's brought me. I'm nervous, too. I never go to work without looking at least somewhat put together. What kind of example would I be setting if I did that?

Opening the overstuffed drawer all of us makeup lovers have, I stare into the abyss of lipsticks, more eyeshadow pallets than I can count on two hands, and every popular must-have mascara, eyeliner, and fancy brush online influencers rave about.

Wasting no time, because I have my makeup routine down to a science, I get to work. Moisturizer first, no foundation. Thanks to a killer nighttime skincare routine, I have gorgeous skin for my age. *Ew.* No. I hate those words. When you're twenty, you never say *for my age*. Once you hit your mid-thirties, it becomes second nature. I don't like it. So, let's make a pact right here and now that neither of us ever say that shit again. *For someone our age.* You mean someone with laugh lines. Someone who has lived a little or a lot. Nope. We're owning our bodies and our style.

I sweep a peachy blush across my cheeks and get to the fun stuff. Adding a smidge of earthy orange shadow to my lid, I deepen it with a rich brown for a smokey eye and finish with a shimmery copper to intensify the look. On goes three swipes of mascara, yes three, thin eyeliner, and a rich, brown lip with a little coppery shimmer in the center.

Giving myself an approving once-over, I blow my reflection a kiss in the mirror and smile.

What a transformation.

I look good, if I do say so myself.

Emboldened to finish today's fashionable look, I use the curling wand that's been cooking in my sink—don't come for me, that's where it goes—to curl the ends of my chest-length hair to add a bit of chunky texture.

With a quick wipe to rid any loose eyeshadow from my face and a dab of a sexy essential oil blend to my pulse points. I tidy up and turn off the curler before heading into the bedroom. In the closet, I snag a brown cardigan off a hanger. It's too damn cold to leave the house with bare arms, and brown fashion boots from the shoe rack.

Alright.

Let's do this thing.

I'm ready.

Running back into the bathroom really quick, I snag a few smaller crystals from my bowl and stuff them into my cardigan pocket for later. Then I make the grand exit—hips swaying with false confidence, my boots *click, click, click* across the hardwood floor, as I join Sunshine in the living room. He's exactly where I said he was, chilling on my couch, booted feet up on my coffee table, ankles crossed.

The moment he looks up from his phone, his eyes round, and he whistles. "Damn, Sweets, you look amazing."

Pressing my lips together as my stomach fizzes from his compliment, I curtsy. It's wobbly and far from graceful, but it draws a warm chuckle from Sunshine as he unfolds from the sofa to stand and stretches both arms above his head, expelling a loud yawn.

"You ready to blow this popsicle stand?" He offers me his hand, palm up, and I clasp mine in his.

"Let's do it."

I snag my purse from the table by the front door on the way out and wait on the porch for Sunshine to lock up, his hand still in mine. Knowing now is as good of time as ever, I fish a crystal from my cardigan and sneak it into his front jeans pocket with a single finger.

Keys jangling from his index finger, Sunshine turns to me. "What d'ya give me today?" His gaze flicks to where his new crystal lives. The bulge is indiscernible through the denim. This isn't my first rodeo. This is how we leave the house together. Our little song and dance. He locks up, and I slide a crystal into his pocket. His work van has an entire cup holder full of my gifts.

"Blue Howlite."

"What's this one for?" he asks as we walk down the porch steps together and over to my newish Bronco parked in the driveway beside his van. Sunshine opens the passenger door for me to climb in. If I'm going anywhere with him, I'm not driving. He won't let me. I lost that battle decades ago. In his mind, women are to be taken care of. Chauffeuring them around is his brand of chivalry, at least in his mind. I don't care either way.

"It's for calm and patience," I explain as I settle into my seat.

His brow furrows. "Because of Dark?"

I set my purse on the floor beside my feet. "Yes… and me."

Cuffing his hand over the top of my open door, Sunshine tilts his head to the side as his expression softens. "Sweets, there's never any reason I need patience 'cause of you. Yeah? You're my home. It's that simple. The Dark shit will sort itself out as it always does. It would be a helluva lot easier if he'd just sign the divorce papers and let you move on with your life."

In that, we agree.

Five sets of divorce papers in eight years, all of them ripped to shreds. The one time I had the courage to file and take him to court, he pulled some sort of magical puppet strings and had it thrown out. Now, I'm still married to a man who's with another woman, and he's still just as stubborn in refusing to divorce me. It's selfish. Everyone knows this. It's been going on for so long that everyone else in our lives besides me, Sunshine, and I'm assuming Abby, because she is his woman, doesn't care. We're just a couple, a non-couple, with a complicated relationship.

Not knowing how to respond, because Sunshine sure has a way of throwing me for an emotional loop, I nod once, and he shuts me in the truck. Rounding the hood, he hops in, fires the engine, and backs us out as I select a rock playlist to jam to on our ten-mile drive to my work.

We're on the road for five minutes, and Sunshine's fingers are tapping on the steering wheel to the beat of "Hotel California", when I finally break the silence.

"What'd you do with the stalker?"

"I made it quick."

Good.

"Through the head?"

"Through the head," he confirms. "It wasn't messy." Easing to a stop, he flicks his blinker on and looks both ways before turning left, past my favorite ice cream shop that's only open when it's warm outside. Their homemade chocolate custard with hot fudge sounds amazing right now. In a cup, with a waffle cone on top, looking a lot like a dunce's cap.

Sunshine catches me staring wistfully at the hot pink building with colorful sprinkles painted on the exterior and chuckles. "It'll open in the spring."

I grumble under my breath. "I wish this would stop happening."

"Which part? The stalkers or the dairy bar bein' closed in the winter?" There's laughter in his voice. Sometimes, he doesn't know how to take me. That makes two of us. Sometimes, I don't know how to take me either.

"Both," I reply, even though I meant the stalker. If they stopped popping up, there wouldn't be any messes to clean up. Don't get me wrong, I don't mind messes. These just feel... pointless—a waste.

"Ya know, that may never happen."

"I know." And I do. I get it. This is my curse. An unwanted gift from my mother. She always had men chasing her. Though, from her own admission, she often opened her legs for them to fulfill her own sexual needs first, only to send them on their way. Unfortunately, they didn't want to go. They wanted more. I never understood why. Not then and surely not now.

"Men want what they can't have, Kali," Sunshine explains. "You're nice to them. A lot of men won't take no for an answer." Reaching across the truck, he pats my knee in reassurance.

No matter how many times we discuss this at length, it never clicks. This isn't the first time, nor will it be the last time, Sunshine and I have this exact conversation.

"He came into the shop every day I was working for over a month." That's how this almost always starts.

"And you treated him like a human being."

That's true. I treat everyone like a human being unless they give me a reason not to. Trust me, there are people who give me a reason not to. Plenty.

"I know," I reply, because what else is there to say?

"You probably smiled and asked him questions, to be polite."

My lips tipped into a frown, I shrug. "He didn't have anybody. His mom died last year. His brother stopped talking to him after that. What was I supposed to do? Be a bitch? Throw him out?"

"Well, he won't be a problem anymore."

No. I guess he won't. Dan was one of the nicer stalkers. They all start out that way. Flirting when they come in to see me. Sometimes, they bring me flowers I refuse to accept. Sometimes, there's more extreme love bombing—money, jewelry, expensive designer bags. Each gift I return, the more adamant they get until they eventually follow me home, take pictures of me through the windows, and masturbate in their cars for me to witness. It's supposed to be flattering, I think.

But it's just sad. This year alone, I've had two stalkers. Last year, three. Similar patterns. Same outcomes. I'm the one who usually handles business. For once, it was nice I didn't have to.

Staring out the side window, watching the world fly by, I sigh at the heaviness of it all. At the heaviness of the day. At the heaviness of… life. "I know you didn't have time to clean up the mess before Lily woke up, so did you call Angel?"

"Yeah. He was closest."

Makes sense. When you need shit done, you call Angel—a Sacred Sinner nomad, just like Dark and Sunshine. He's a close, personal friend. Reliable and efficient. The stalker's blue sedan is probably in a chop shop by now, pieced down for parts. His body, however, they handle the bodies. I don't ask questions. It's none of my business. Just as what I do isn't theirs. We respect those boundaries.

Pulling out my phone from inside my purse, I find Angel's number in my contacts.

Me: Thanks for your help today.

Angel: Never a problem. I'm always here for you, gorgeous. Whatever you need. Hit me up yourself next time. Yeah?

Head shaking from the driver's seat, Sunshine snickers as he turns down the town's main street not far from the shop. "You're texting Angel to thank him, aren't you?"

"It's the right thing to do, Colton," I scold playfully. "Just as I'm gonna thank you, probably a thousand times, once I get my gift gifts."

"Sweets…" My nickname's drawled on a sigh, one that

communicates me thanking him is unnecessary. That's where he'd be wrong.

"What? It's true. You should already know that."

"I do. But it's unnecessary."

See. Told ya.

I hum in disagreement as Sunshine drives past the shop and turns up the next alley to park behind the building—the employee's entrance.

At the back of the old brick building, there are two doors—one at the street level where the stores are and another that goes down a small flight of steps beneath the main spaces.

Sunshine kills the engine.

I unlatch my seatbelt and turn toward him.

He reaches out and lays a warm hand on my knee. "They should be downstairs."

I rest my palm on top of the skull tattoo on the back of his hand. "Thank you."

The corner of his mouth kicks into the sweetest of grins, crinkling the edges of his eyes that sparkle in the early afternoon sun. "I want what's best for you. Always." He squeezes my knee.

Returning the gesture in kind, I squeeze the top of his hand. "I know. Now I'm gonna go see my gift gifts, and you go upstairs." I jut my chin toward the back door of the building. "Till should be working. She'll be happy to see you."

"If you need me—"

"I know."

"I mean it."

"I know you do."

"I'm not leavin' 'til morning."

"I sure as hell hope not. You'd miss the party."

Sunshine laughs, deep and rumbly. It settles something in me as it always has. "Well, alrighty then."

With a final pat on the back of his hand, I grab my purse from the floor and exit the truck. As I descend the basement steps, Sunshine enters through the rear of the shop, no doubt to be greeted by his biggest fans.

Pausing at the steel door, the camera does its standard scan. Recognizing me, the lock disengages, and I pull the handle to go inside.

The warmth from the heater, steeped with the scent of vanilla and baked goods, wafts in my face, drawing a smile to the surface as I wade into our base—the safe house, ground zero for our operations. I set my purse on the metal console table by the entrance of the great room that unfurls into an old-school office space like the ones you see in those noir detective films—wainscoting, cream walls, and sectioned-off rooms with brass-handled doors that have windows, some of them frosted for privacy. The wood accents and well-preserved brick exterior walls add a rich layer of coziness to the entire space.

There's a wall of whiteboards and a wall of newspaper clippings pinned to cork—trophies for the women of a job well done. In the center of the main living space is a family-sized table, large enough to seat twelve and up to sixteen if you squeeze in like sardines. Two familiar faces look up from eating as I approach, each of them smiling.

"Hey, boss." Dina waves her spoon in hello before diving back into her bowl of cereal.

Sam, the quiet one, two-finger waves.

I scan the room, looking for what I came down here for—to meet and greet. That is my job, after all. This is my place.

When Dina notices me linger, she points her spoon to the far side of the room, where Cell works her computer hacker magic in a deep alcove once used as a hallway.

Standing behind our resident smarty pants are two heads I don't recognize, watching one of Cell's five screens lit up with a shit load of information about various groups and people we keep tabs on around the country.

They say nothing as she points animatedly to a set of six black-and-white photos she throws up on the screen. One of them is the infamous sex trafficker, Remy Whitaker. He's the reason almost all of these women are here today, apart from myself.

"That's him." She gestures to the tatted-out male in the center—full beard, big muscles, screwed-up expression. The other photos are of his top dogs. The men who are just as bad as him—if not worse. He runs his enterprise from an ivory tower, swimming in money from the sale of humans. While those assholes are on the ground, running auctions, or worse, baby factories, where they sedate pregnant women at the end of their third trimester, deliver the babies, and dispose of the mother's corpses like they were yesterday's trash. Vile doesn't even begin to put a name to what they do. Those newborns are part of an underground adoption system for sickos and rich pricks alike.

When Cell gets through with her colorful explanation of the douchiest of douchebags, her words, not mine, I clear my throat to let them know I'm present.

"Oh, shit." Cell giggles and blushes ten shades of pink as she shoots up from her chair and sends it flying into the wall. "H-hey, Boss Lady, how long you been standing there?" She retrieves the runaway seat and throws herself into it, sending it and herself back under the edge of her desk.

"Long enough." I wink in her direction as the two women Sunshine delivered turn to face me.

These are the gift gifts I was going on about.

His presents to me.

The one not much taller than me, at my below-average five foot four, is curvy, with long blonde hair and a heart-shaped cherub face. She smiles much like Cell does, full of life.

The other woman, a thin brunette who looks very much like your average girl next door, wrings her finger in front of her as she chews on her bottom lip, refusing to make eye contact. Alright, so this one is shy and was probably tortured a time or two. That's normal around these parts. I know it's messed up, but these women are here because of their histories. It's molded them into what we need for our operations—intel. That's what we do. We get in, we get information, we get out. Occasionally, some sisters, that's what we call ourselves, go undercover, assimilate, build relationships with the scum of the earth, and deliver information by means that put them in a direct line of danger. I used to be one of them. Others, Cell, in particular, prefer to work behind the scenes—away from the bad men.

"Hello, ladies, I'm Kali." Keeping my distance out of respect for what they've gone through, I wave to the ladies and smile. It's genuine. I'm glad they're here.

"She's our boss," Cell chimes in from her chair as she spins around in it like a child, and I good-naturedly roll my eyes. I'm not anyone's boss, not in the militant, you-better-follow-my-orders nonsense. We're a family here—end of discussion.

Undeterred, I continue my introduction. "I'm sure being here is a little scary with all you've been through. So, why don't you two follow me?" I sweep my hand toward the great room. "I'll show you around your new home and get you settled into your rooms."

Wanting to have a little one-on-one with the ladies, away from the rest of the sisters, I show them around their new underground home that runs half the block beneath the storefronts. The ceilings are tall, industrial, and painted black. The lighting is soft, with none of those harsh fluorescents to worry about.

In the main space, we pass Sam and Dina, still at the table eating.

They wave but say nothing.

The women return their gestures in kind.

Off to the furthest side is the communal living room, with three overstuffed couches and a giant television mounted on the brick wall.

The kitchen is a hop, skip, and a jump from there, tucked into an old, spacious office supply room. Thanks to the help of the Sacred Sinners, it's industrial, with all the bells and whistles you could ever want—a massive double-sided fridge and matching freezer, a steel table that runs the center of the room as a prep space and makeshift island, and an open shelf where they store all the bigger kitchen gadgets.

On the counter, Till left a plate full of chocolate chip and double chocolate cookies—my favorite. I snatch one up and scoot the plate to the edge. "Have at 'em," I encourage the ladies.

The blonde accepts a double chocolate like mine as the brunette declines with a meek shake of the head. By the looks of her, I'm guessing she doesn't eat much. Eating disorders come with the territory here, as do mental health problems. We have a therapist most of these women see via telehealth. It's mandatory at first and after assignments.

Out of the communal space, we enter a hallway lined with former offices—all of them have wooden doors, brass knobs, and frosted windows. Crisp white numbers adorn their fronts. Number two houses the laundry. Three is a storage room. Four and five spans two large offices converted into a bathroom. Multiple white subway-tiled shower stalls flank one side with curtains for privacy. In the center, there are sinks with mirrors mounted above them on the brick wall that separates the shower area from the row of toilet stalls. Along the back wall are hooks and a row of short lockers for the sisters to store their stuff. It has your standard college dorm vibe, but that's what they sign up for. Nothing about this is forced. It's an option they're given from where they once came. Yes, I know that's vague. I don't know their backstories, only that in order to be here, you've had to have gone through some shit. Ugly shit. Then have gone through extensive therapy and rehabilitation to be welcomed back into the real world.

Cell was sold as a child to some rich fuck and found as a teenager when she escaped. By some miracle, she ran into the right bikers outside a truck stop one night. She's open about her lived experiences, as it helps many of the new sisters feel welcome and at ease. The newbies have probably been hanging with her since they arrived. She's that fun, over-the-top kid sister everyone doesn't want but needs in their life.

Once we've hit all the common areas, I show the ladies to their new bedrooms. I keep each room stocked and ready for any of Sunshine's unexpected visits. He's not one to give me a heads-up, as he rarely knows about the pickups until hours before I do. That doesn't leave much time to communicate in the middle of the night, which is when they always arrive, under the guise of dark, just in case any of the fuckers who try to keep tabs on the Sacred Sinners follow.

Opening the side-by-side doors, I sweep my hand for the women to enter whichever room they prefer. They're clones of each other, much like a hotel room—full-sized bed, white sheets, fluffy white duvet, brand-new pillows, a dresser with a small television on top, a short rod mounted to the wall with hangers, a mini-fridge, and a small cupboard area with a sink, and just enough counter space for a microwave. The walls are white, and the floor is hardwood with a small area rug for warmth.

"Welcome to your new home," I announce. "Whenever you're ready, I'd like us to talk in the living room."

With that, I give them space to settle in as I happy dance all the way to the common room and dramatically fall onto the couch, ousting a ridiculously loud squeal.

I have new sisters.

New women to bring into the fold.

I'm so damn excited!

Sunshine is getting all the hugs for this—all the thank yous and rocks for his pockets.

Leaving her little corner, Cell drops on the couch across from me, as does Dina. Sam disappears, which is what Sam does best. If I didn't know the woman, I wouldn't know she lived here. She's a ghost most of the time. It's a miracle she was eating at the table when I arrived.

Righting myself on the sofa, I fold my hands into my lap, all prim and proper and shit. "I love it when we get new sisters."

"I know! This is fun. I wonder what they'll think of the

rest of us. I hope they fit in. I'm sure they will. Bonez wouldn't send them here without knowing they'd work. He's smart," Cell yammers faster than a subway train.

"That's true, and with Rosie now vetting everyone first, I'm sure they'll work out for the best." I sit back on the couch. It's so deep my feet come off the floor.

"Bongo sent so many new opportunities for us to work our magic this week." Cell rubs her hands together like a bad guy in a movie.

"I don't know if they're ready for fieldwork yet. They just got here."

"But you said Rosie already met them," she counters.

This is true. Rosie is our unofficial badass sister from the south. Having worked in the thick of things with the sex trafficking world for years, she gets the final say in who joins us. For the longest time, the Sacred Sinners sent us too many women. One out of five would stick around long enough to get into the field. Most were sent back into the real world. You may think you want to work intel to make a difference, but it can be a dark and scary place. If you were one of those taken for a long time, beaten, raped, or tortured, you might not want to be anywhere near that world, no matter the cost or the reward, and there's no shame in that. This lifestyle isn't for everyone.

"Did they give you their names?" I ask Cell.

Her mop of blonde curls shakes. "I didn't ask. Sunshine's buzzer thingy rang early this morning. I let them in, and they slept on the couches most of the morning. I just got them up and talking right before you got here."

"It doesn't matter anyhow," Dina interjects, tucking herself into the corner of the couch as she picks her nails with the tip of a pocketknife. "We get to choose our names. Cell isn't your real name, just as Dina isn't mine."

"True. True." Cell nods along enthusiastically. "I was kept in a cell. It seemed fitting to have a name that reminded me of that."

"You're a morbid bitch." Dina snickers, and I grin at the fact that, yes, Cell is indeed a morbid bitch to the core. I don't think anyone could do the job she does if they weren't.

Owning who she is, Cell raises the roof old-school style as her shoulders swivel in an awkward wannabe dance. "That I am, sister. That. I. Am," she sings.

Before long, we are joined by the two newbies. They sit beside each other on the last couch. The brunette stares at her fingers as the blonde forces a tight smile.

"How'd you like your rooms?" I ask, hoping to make this transition as easy as possible. You don't ask too many questions with new sisters. You keep it light. You give them all the information they need to settle in and cross your fingers that they trust you enough to open up in the coming weeks. Most of them find a sister or two to bond with. From the looks of things, these two will be a unit, much like Till and me.

"The room's nice," the blonde answers as the brunette remains impassive.

"Good. Good. I assume you met with Rosie before coming here?"

"Yes." The blonde presses her lips together and nods. "She briefed us about this place and taught us some self-defense."

"How long were you there?" Cell asks, ever the nosy nelly.

Eyebrows raised in warning, I stare her down for pushing too far too fast, but Cell shrugs as if she's not being invasive.

"I got there a few days before Beth." The blonde bumps shoulders with her companion. "We were there about a month."

Navigating away from Rosie talk, I focus on something else instead, like introductions. "It's nice to meet you, Beth… and…" I pause and smile at the talkative one, waiting for her to fill in the blank.

"Oh." The blonde giggles, fingers fluttering at her chest in embarrassment. "Sorry. I'm Destiny."

"Are those your real names?" Cell cuts in, hands flailing as if she's got a million things to say and can't get them out fast enough. "Because I'm sure you've been told you don't have to keep those. Some sisters feel better getting a whole new identity when they come into this world. Do you want a new identity? It's okay if you don't. We won't judge you. Kali's just Kali. She was named after a goddess. Her ex-husband Dark, you'll meet him sometime, he's kind of grumpy. Oh, and Sunshine, who's her ex-father-in-law, friend, whatever…" The motormouth waves her words off. "He's the hot guy who dropped you off this morning. They have Kali tattoos. Of the Goddess, not her. Well. I mean, I guess they're her, too—"

"Cell," I interject. "Breathe."

Hunched forward on the couch, she nods on repeat like a bobblehead doll, drawing in a deep, audible breath.

Damn. That's far more information than these women need to know now or ever. If you're wondering, which I am sure you are, thanks to Cell's big mouth…Yes, my name is Kali. Yes, I was named after what she said I was. Yes, my ex and his father have tattoos of her in honor of me. No, I didn't know about them until after they got them done. Both have the Goddess tattooed on their left side, spanning from armpit to hip in full color. That's all I'll say about it. It was a long time ago. They made stupid choices I see every time they have their shirts off. I try not to notice, but it's hard to miss when the Hindu Goddess is depicted in blue, has multiple arms, her tongue sticking out, and looks like a total badass, which is why my mother named me after her. Kali is the Hindu Goddess of death and rebirth, embodying the power of creation and destruction in one entity, transcending good and evil. She is Mother Nature. She is the Goddess of time. So basically, she's the baddest of bad bitches.

Dina snorts at Cell's enthusiasm. Yeah. That's what we'll call it. I wonder how much caffeine our resident smarty pants had this morning. Knowing her, it was an entire pot of coffee.

Unfazed by our lively sister, the blonde continues the conversation as if she caught everything Cell gushed. "Oh. Yes. I know. My name's not really Destiny. When I was rescued from a barn a couple of years ago, I didn't want to be the old me. Bonez said it was okay."

"It is," I confirm, not knowing what else to say. I smooth down the side of my skirt.

A tear slips down Beth's cheek and plops onto her lap. "I don't want to be Beth anymore. I don't want to be her anymore." She swipes the back of her hand across her face to clear the wetness, and my heart aches for her.

"Hey. That's totally fine. I know this is a lot to take in. You won't have to do anything you don't want to ever again."

Beth nods along to my words, her movements jerky as if she's deep inside her head, floating in a world of unpleasant emotions. Also, normal. This takes a lot to process. New surroundings. A whole new life. A new job.

"Dina and Cell will be here anytime you need something.... and those stairs..." My words are soft as I point to the corner of the room. "Lead up to the shop. You're welcome to visit anytime during open hours. Many of the women you probably saw milling about this morning work there during the day. They'll show you around, and next week, or whenever you're ready, they'll walk you through your responsibilities up there."

The women listen intently as I fill in whatever they need to know. Every sister has a job here, whether that's working in the store, cleaning the apartment like Dina does, or nerding out like Cell. We are a family. We support the others. To drive that point home, Cell gets up and grabs a box of tissues. She hands them to Beth before returning to her spot on the couch.

For however long it takes, I sit back and talk to Destiny and Beth. I answer any questions they may have. Cell chimes in as she always does, and Dina adds whatever I might have missed. When the women finally relax, their tears become a distant memory. When the smiles come naturally, and they seem to breathe easier, that's my cue to be done for the day.

Sliding to the edge of the couch, I look each sister in the eye long enough to connect, but not too long that I make it weird. "We're having a party upstairs tonight. You're welcome to join if you'd like."

Leaving them to their own devices, I climb the steps to join Sunshine at the shop, where Till is likely talking his ear off or trying to get into his pants. You never know what you'll get with those two.

FIVE

With a wine glass half full of the most delicious, aged port, my hips and skirt sway to the beat of "Witchy Woman" as I nibble on another piece of dark chocolate. It melts on my tongue, coating my palate. I groan at how fucking decadent it is.

The world fades as the beat flows through me.

I am it.

It is me.

My eyes slide closed as I revel in the freedom without a care in the world. Today was a good day, even after a questionable morning.

Big hands and even bigger arms envelop me from behind as the familiar scent of pine and citrus reaches my nose. A chin rests on my shoulder. Hot breath warms my ear as my hair's tucked around the shell.

"Hello, gorgeous." A lingering kiss rests upon the side of my neck as splayed fingers press into my belly, each one a brand upon flesh. I burn for this, for him, for his touch, for the attention. I need it.

And he knows.

He knows exactly what I need.

We sway to the song and the next, lost in time.

When I open my eyes to take another sip of port, Sunshine's there, watching me from his stool at the bar, getting his fill of local craft beer we supply just for him.

My best friend, Till, waves from her spot behind the bar. My drunken smile lifts at the corner as I salute her and Sunshine with my glass.

Running a hand through his thick gray hair, Sunshine smiles tightly and salutes me in return as the pair of hands at my belly slide down to my hips and back to my stomach again, stoking a fire I'll need to quench.

"I missed you," he rasps in my ear.

"I missed you, too," I whisper in return.

Patrons mill about the room, some drinking, some eating, and some dancing. Destiny and Beth sit at a small table in the corner with Cell, sharing a bottle of wine, immersed in what seems like a fun conversation that brings a faint smile to Beth's lips.

The front door opens, and the air shifts.

The hair on my arms stand on end as the electricity in the room charges. Sunshine's eyes narrow into tiny slits, glaring just past me.

Sensing him as I always do, the invisible tether draws tight—Dark. Just when I was having fun, just when I was relaxing and letting the alcohol flow, he has to show his face—the fun sucker.

The hands at my waist are replaced by a fully tattooed arm wrapped around my middle in protection. The body behind me stiffens. "That motherfucker," my companion rumbles, and I laugh, maniacal and crazy at the absurdity of it all.

When your husband cheats on you, you take time to cry and wallow, but then you quit being a baby, and you host a party. You enjoy yourself. You appreciate what you have now and how far you've come. When the sadness creeps in, because it always does… You remember the times he left his dirty crew socks just outside the hamper for you to pick up. You remember the ugly fights. You remember the days he promised to mow the grass but never did, so you had to. You remember the kids' plays he missed because he was gone. You remember the piles of Kleenex on the floor from hours of sobbing, nose raw, eyes swollen shut, skin dry and blotchy. You remember picking up the pieces of your broken life.

That's why you party.

To celebrate yourself.

That is what we're doing.

What *I'm* doing.

The first few years were tough—sitting at home with Sunshine and Till, eating popcorn, watching a movie, and sometimes getting drunk.

This was Till's brilliant idea.

No more giving Dark power.

Now, we host a tasting night on the same date each year.

Wine and chocolate.

The perfect combination.

Here is my life's work—a dual shop. One side is a winery that Till runs that also serves spirits. The other is a chocolate shop, where Sugar and her posse of chocolatiers and bakers whip up the highest-quality sweets.

Both women have been my sidekicks for over a decade—

building our businesses and our not-so-little underground network together as partners, sisters, and friends.

Dark Delicacies is our home away from home.

Yes, I was the fool who named my shop after my now ex.

Do I regret it?

Sometimes.

Until we have days like today when our friends and community come out to celebrate with us.

At the door, Dina collects the cover charge and hands out the sip and snack tickets—three treats to pair with three wines.

The pairings are spread on circular high-top tables throughout the interconnected shops, with white, handwritten cards in the center, explaining the choice of wine, and it's paired sweet, artfully curated by Till and Sugar for this evening.

Dark hasn't crashed our party in ages.

Transfixed on the swirl of red liquid in my glass, I do what I always do in Dark's presence—pretend he's not there. It works for half a song until my dance partner curses, and another set of feet drop into view as I stare down at the refinished hardwood floor. I know those boots—worn leather, a scuff on the right toe from a bar fight. I also know those legs, clad in dark denim, and that wide stance.

"Kali." My name's a prayer upon his lips.

I heave a sigh.

"Kali." His tone sharpens.

My grip on the glass stem tightens.

The arm around my waist turns into a band of steel as it lifts all of me off the floor as if I weigh nothing and slowly backs away.

"Angel. Put my fuckin' wife down," Dark seethes, taking a

step forward, fists clenching and unclenching down at his sides.

"Not your wife, *pendejo*," my savior grumbles.

I snicker, and Dark's jaw ticks as he advances on us. Knowing a scene is about to go down, Sunshine's out of his stool in a flash, inserting himself between Dark and me. Till opens the door to the hall, and Angel carries me through the back and into the office, where he sets me back on the ground. Till's hot on our tail, shutting us inside and leaving Sunshine to handle his son.

"That selfish motherfucker." Till paces the room, hands balled down at her sides. If this were a cartoon movie, steam would billow from her ears.

Angel, being the biggest man in a fifty-mile radius, sets up shop in front of the closed door and crosses his arms until his biceps, the size of my head, look like they might explode in repressed anger. His lip curls up in disgust as he leans all his weight against the steel. Nobody's getting past him unless he wants them to.

Barely fazed by this entire ordeal, I hitch my ass on the edge of the basic office desk I share with Till and cross my ankles. "That's not at all how I saw tonight going."

Drinking my memories away and ending the night with a fat cock courtesy of Angel… Yep, that's how I wanted things to go. It's been months since I last got laid. If you haven't already caught on… I don't date much. Staying busy with the shop, Lily, or the sisters leaves me little time to do the whole get-to-know-someone, and at forty, what's the point? I know that makes me sound like a sad sack Sally. But it's true. So, I meet a random man off the street, date him, and then what? He finds out my invasive, far-too-hot-for-his-own-good ex and my… Sunshine, the equally sexy but less douchy of a man, are bikers. If that's not enough to scare them off, how about the other stuff? Like… me. I'm weird enough to put average men off, or in the case of the stalkers, weird enough to find me appealing enough to stalk. Make it make sense. When you figure it out, let me know.

"What do you wanna do about this, Kali?" Till stops her pacing long enough to thumb toward the door.

Toying with my glass, I shrug and consume my last sip of port. "What's there *to* do?"

"Kill him," Angel suggests unhelpfully, his lips spreading into a cruel smile.

"I love that idea," Till adds. Of course, she does. She's Dark's sworn enemy. Not that he cares all that much. Till's all tits and spicy personality. She talks a big game, but she's no killer.

My eyes roll so far into the back of my head that I can see what I ate yesterday for lunch. "Neither of you actually want him dead."

Angel grumbles, knowing I'm right.

Till returns the sentiment.

See.

There's a knock at the door. "It's me." *Sunshine.*

"He gone?" Angel asks.

"Nope."

An entire short story of Spanish expletives flies from Angel's mouth. Bitch and asshole are a few colorful additions I pick up, but the rest I can't understand.

Till takes the wine glass from my hand and gestures for me to get off the desk. I swing my legs, hop down with flair, and approach the door, where Angel stands guard. If Sunshine couldn't get Dark to leave and Dark was here for me, that means he's got something he needs to say that can't wait until tomorrow. Or he thinks can't wait until tomorrow. That's far more likely.

Knowing the dicking down isn't gonna happen tonight, I grip what I can of Angel's forearm in apology. "You know I gotta talk to him."

Angel's nostrils flare.

"Thanks for coming to see me tonight."

Shoulders deflating, Angel's chin drops to his chest as he nods just once. His almost black eyes latch on to mine. "I got you, gorgeous. Anytime. Yeah?"

Lifting onto my tippy toes, I press my body against Angel's and lean up enough to plant a quick kiss on his cheek. "You're the best."

An innocent smile curves at the corner of Angel's mouth as pink suffuses his brown cheeks. Without asking him to, he slides out of the way of the door and lets me pass.

"Give him hell!" Till cheers at my retreating back as I join Sunshine in the hall.

I flash her a thumbs-up over my shoulder. "Where is he?" I address my favorite guy. "This had damn well better be important."

Without answering my question, Sunshine's gentle hand presses to the small of my back. Its supportive heat radiates through my cardigan as he escorts me through the bar and out front, where Dark leans against his Harley, illuminated by a streetlamp.

The air's crisp. Steam plumes from my lips as I rub my arms up and down, wondering why in the hell we need to have this conversation outside when my nipples have already turned into painful rocks.

"Be nice," Sunshine warns his son before he leans down, drops a simple kiss on my temple, and disappears back inside, where he can drink, stay warm, and doesn't have to look his son in the face. Lucky him.

"What do you want, Dark?" I inquire when he doesn't break the silence, though his eyes do. They say everything. He rakes my form from head to toe. His slow, shivery gaze drinks its fill. This is another reason I hate being around him. This is what Dark does. He gives zero fucks. He stares if he wants to stare. He shows up unannounced and unwanted and lives his life, however it works for him. Who cares how I feel… How Abby feels.

He's an asshole.

When I open my mouth to tell him just that, a grin kicks up at the corner of his perfect lips. "I miss you."

My expression twists into a hideous scowl. "Fuck right off."

Dark throws his head back, and his hardy laugh booms into the night. "God, you're fuckin' perfect."

Please excuse me while I roll my eyes. "What do you want?" I snip.

"Like right now? Or—"

"You know what I mean," I cut in. "Why are you here?"

"Ah. Yes. That." Dark's fingers tap a staccato beat on this thigh, like he's nervous, or there's a song playing in his head he can't quite shake.

"Yes. That." I gesture for him to get on with it. Because at this rate, I'll turn into a popsicle in T-minus ten minutes.

His chin lifts toward the store. "Do you wanna go inside to talk?"

Hell, to the no. "I want you to tell me why you're here so I can go back inside and you can go home, where you belong. Stop stalling."

Dark nods once and gets on with it. "I got a call tonight

from someone in the club. You know I can't say who, but they didn't want to run this through Cell."

"Okay. And?" That still doesn't explain what that has to do with me.

"They have a job."

"*Annnd?*" Impatiently tapping my foot on the sidewalk, I rub my palms up and down my arms for warmth as my fingers prickle from the cold.

"It's for you."

I figured as much, or why else would he be here?

"*Annnd?*" I stare at him pointedly, needing him to reach the point now, not in fifteen years.

"It's for three weeks, maybe longer."

Sheesh, could he be any more evasive?

"What's the job, Dark? Spit it out. I'm fucking freezing here." To prove my point, I blow smoke into the cool air like a dragon.

Brow furrowing in the center, my ex stands to his full height, shrugs off his leather jacket, and hands it over for me to put on. I don't question it because I don't want him inside to have this chat. I also want to stop shivering. Throwing it on, it's so damn big it almost touches my knees. My hands hide in the depths of the arms, like a small child wearing their father's clothes. I look like an idiot, but I don't care. Thankfully, my shaking quickly ceases because he warmed the inside, and we are not gonna discuss how much it smells like him. It's like a Dark burrito—warm and fragrant. It's bliss and hell in equal measure.

Dark pulls a hoodie from his saddlebag and throws it on before he retakes his bike. Probably so we're eye-to-eye, and he appears less intimidating at this level. If that's the case, it's working.

"Thanks." I press my lips together in a tight smile. "Now, about this job." I don't ask if this could have waited until morning because we both know it could have. My guess is he just got the call and left to see me. Not thinking is one of Dark's strong suits.

He stuffs his hands inside the front pocket of his hoodie. "It's in California, on the coast. We need to establish your presence there. You'll be working on a yacht as a maid, server, or whatever they need from you."

I nod along.

Dark continues, "At the end of the month, the yacht is set to have a party, two nights on the open seas, international waters. There will be guests. Rich pricks like you've dealt with before and women."

"It's another auction, isn't it?" I guess, having encountered them before.

"Yes," he confirms.

"How many?"

"Right now. Ten women, high dollar. Twelve men."

Of course, it is.

"Let me guess. They want new hires for the yacht because, after the auction, they plan to kill the newbies and dump them overboard. Or, they plan to sell them to the other men as consolation prizes to stroke their bruised egos." Fucking disgusting.

"Bingo." The man winks at me. Fucking winks. "You know your shit, babe." Dark's sumptuous mouth splits into a blinding smile, all-white teeth, and a dimple. To make matters worse, his penetrating gaze sears into me, stripping me bare right here on the sidewalk.

I hate it.

My stomach pitches at the unwanted attention. I don't

want praise from him. I don't want anything from him. A job is a job. That's fine. I can do a job. This… this I can't do.

"This isn't my first rodeo," I grumble. It's lame, but it's true. I've been in this world so long, nothing surprises me anymore. They kidnap women, break them, and then sell them to the highest bidders across the globe as subservient pets. It's just another cash cow for the rich fucks of the world. You would be shocked by the number of billionaires who make extra money peddling flesh.

"Well." Dark clears his throat and schools his features. "It kinda is, 'cause I'm gonna be one of the bidders."

Dammit.

There's the catch.

"Is that why you've been gone a lot lately?" I ask.

"Oh. So, you noticed. I'm touched." Dark grasps his heart dramatically and swoons.

"Shut it. Lily has been over more than usual. That means you've been gone." Normally, she visits a few times a week. For the last couple of months, it's been pretty much every day. An hour here. An hour there. I try not to notice anything about Dark if I can avoid it. That makes life easier.

"I've got three months in on this, building my relationship to get a seat at the table. Darmond Cassiano is running the show."

Damn.

I whistle, impressed. "He's a big fish."

"No. Babe. He's a goddamn whale. If we take him out, his California connections and crew will scramble to find a replacement. That'll leave a big enough window for our guys to put a world of hurt on 'em."

He's right. This is huge. If this works, more women will be saved, and another pillar will be ripped right out from under Remy's operations. If one of his big dogs gets put down, there's no telling how quickly his empire will crumble. After the shit this man has done to my sisters, I'm happy to knock him down as far as I can until someone puts a bullet between his eyes.

"Fine," I yield.

"You'll do it?" Dark's eyes light up like a kid on Christmas morning. I don't know why he sounds surprised. He knows me. He knows what I'll do to save women and put assholes to ground.

"Yes, but you already knew that."

"Not this time, I didn't. 'Cause I'm involved. I figured you'd let someone else step in."

"You don't scare me, Dark. I just don't like you." Which is mostly true.

"No. You love me."

I shake my head at his level of ridiculousness. "In your dreams."

"Every night." He winks again, and out pops those charming dimples.

Smiling, despite his arrogance, I snort. "You're impossible."

"Kali. For real. I'm sorry about everything. You know this. I also know me showin' up this morning was fucked. I know you and Pops have a solid relationship. It tears me up in here sometimes." Dark taps the center of his chest with two fingers.

"All the time," I counter.

"Yeah. All the time," he agrees with a nod. "I fuckin' hate he gets to be close to you, but I can't."

"You made that choice. I didn't."

"I know."

"Then stop takin' it out on me. I've accepted you're my neighbor. I love Lily. I've tried time and time again to be friendly with Abby, but she hates my guts, and I don't blame her for that. I don't take it too personally. Showing up here to tell me this tonight, when it could have waited until morning, was low, Dark. I was in there with my friends having fun." I point to the storefront behind me.

"You were gonna fuck Angel again," he growls.

"Yes. I was." There's no use in denying it. I'm a single woman. I can have relations with whoever I want—end of story. I won't be cowed. Not by him. Not by anyone.

Standing to his full height, Dark clenches his jaw, blows out the world's longest breath, and unfurls smoke into the sky. "Christ, Kali, I don't want you fuckin' Angel. He's my goddamn brother, and you're my wife."

"I'm only your wife by paperwork, Dark. Stop that shit." I'm tired of this. At some point, he has to let it go. Move on. I have.

"No. I sure as fuck won't. I love you." To prove his point, Dark lifts his hand to show me his wedding ring. The same ring I slid on his finger the day we married at the park. We were kids then. I was still a teenager. It was three days after I earned my GED. The rings weren't top-of-the-line, but they were matching white-gold bands with an intricate carving—a gift from Sunshine. That was so long ago. It feels like another life.

To pound into his head that we aren't on the same page, I raise my left arm and push down the jacket sleeve to show him what he already knows. There's no ring on my finger. I took it off the week after he returned with Abby and Lily. It's stored in a velvet bag in the top drawer of my dresser, with all the other keepsakes.

Needing to stay on task and away from our relationship status, I focus on why he's interrupting my night in the first place. "Send me the details when you have them. I'll give the sisters a heads-up that I'll be gone a while." To get back to the tasting, I shrug off Dark's coat and return it to its owner.

Said owner shakes his head, pushing my hand away. "Keep it. Give it back to me in the morning when I drop by to talk about the details of our trip."

"This isn't *our* anything, Dark." I throw the jacket onto the back of his bike seat and pivot on my heel to get the hell away from him.

"See you in the morning, wifey," he calls to my retreating form.

Fuck him.

I flip my ex the bird as Dina opens the door from the inside to welcome me back. His responding boom of laughter sends an eerie chill down my spine.

I dunno what I just agreed to, but I sure as hell hope I don't live to regret it.

All my family's eyes are on me as I stroll back into my shop, checking to see if I'm okay. That's what matters. Them. What we've made together. As I join Sunshine at the bar, my heart grows three whole sizes, just like the Grinch.

No words are exchanged as he draws me between his spread legs and cups my face in his hands. Our gazes meet, and he waits for me to speak. His breath is warm and soaked in rich beer as it wafts across my face. I drink him in—his kindness, the concern etched across his forehead, his… just *him*. It's hard to explain, so I won't even try.

"You ready to go home, Sweets? Or you wanna dance with me?"

The song changes to "Wonderful Tonight" by Eric Clapton.

Sunshine doesn't await my reply when he removes his hands from my face, stands, and pulls me to the center of the room, to our makeshift dancefloor on nights like tonight. Till, being Till, lowers the overhead lights as I sway to the beat of one of my favorite songs, in the arms of the only person who makes me feel safe.

My head rests against Sunshine's upper chest, where his heartbeat thrums in my ear. Wrapping both arms around him, I grip the bottom of his shirt, close my eyes, and expel a pent-up breath I've been holding onto for what feels like hours.

Fingers sift through the back of my hair, and Sunshine holds me close, humming Clapton low enough only I can hear. It's perfection. Just what I need.

When we head home for the night, Sunshine drives with his hand in mine. We don't speak. There's nothing to be said.

At home, in the comfort of my bedroom, I slip on a pair of shorts and a crop top as Sunshine strips down to his boxers. Again, we say nothing as I crawl onto my side of the bed and he on his.

We meet in the middle. His warm skin envelops mine as I become the small spoon to his bigger. My ass to his crotch.

Just like that, we sleep.

And I'm safe.

SIX

There's no mouthwatering French toast or bacon perfuming the house as I peel my eyes open, but there's heat and a hard cock pressed against my ass. Hot breath tickles my neck as my bed companion snores lightly. Sunshine's hand has somehow migrated from my stomach to cup my breast. I peer down at the tattooed hand and mash my lips together to keep from laughing. This isn't the first time this has happened. The last time I teased him about it, he turned fifty shades of embarrassed. It was one of the sweetest reactions I've ever seen. This man would never cross any lines unless we discussed them at length first.

It took years for us to agree to sleep in bed together whenever he visits. It was my idea, partly because I've always loved having a bed partner to sleep and cuddle with and because he's Sunshine. Who wouldn't want to sleep with him in bed?

The world's lightest fingernail *tap, tap, tap* sounds at my bedroom door, followed by a church mouse whisper.

Smiling wide, I tuck the blanket further up my chest so

our little visitor doesn't get an eyeful of half-naked Pops in bed, getting his boob feelers on in his unconscious state.

"Come in," I whisper.

The door creeps open, and her adorable face appears as she tiptoes inside, wearing a pair of unicorn pajamas, her hair still a wild mess from a good night's sleep. I pat the spot on the mattress over the blanket. Nodding excitedly for snuggle time, Lily climbs into the spot, facing me.

Tucking a lock of dark hair around the shell of her ear, I press a finger to my lips to signal we gotta be quiet so we don't wake Pops.

She nods and claps a little hand over her mouth to keep from giggling, but her eyes brighten, and I catch a sweet grin peek out from behind her fingers.

The man at my back grumbles.

I freeze, not wanting to rouse him.

Lily's eyes round to the size of hubcaps.

Do you think we should wake him? I mouth to her.

Somehow reading my lips, Lily's head shakes just as footsteps resonate outside my now open bedroom door.

I die a little inside.

Dark's here.

On days I know I'm not going anywhere and think Lily might want to come over, I leave the back door unlocked. I guess Dark took that as an invitation.

I motion to the door.

Lily mouths what I think is the word, *Dad*, which confirms my suspicions. He said he was coming to discuss our new job, but I didn't think it would be this early. The clock on my nightstand reads a little after eight. Yep. This is way too early on a Sunday to deal with my ex.

As if things couldn't get worse, said dark-haired, gray-eyed man, saunters straight into my bedroom in a pair of gray sweatpants outlining his *you-know-what* and a comfy, long-sleeve t-shirt. Taking one look at my bed, he opens his mouth like he's about to lose his fucking mind, and just as I expect him to curse, the body behind me jostles, rubs his still erect cock against my ass, and rumbles, "Go to the fuckin' livin' room, Dark."

My stomach dips.

The hand tightens around my breast.

"Pops, you're awake!" Lily cheers, wiggling on the bed, oblivious to the awkward situation unfolding.

"Lily," Dark grumbles and thrusts his hand out for his daughter to join him. "We'll be in the living room whenever you two finish doing whatever the fuck this is."

Following her father's orders, Lily pecks my cheek and scrambles to join Dark. Her much smaller hand is consumed by his as they depart and shut the door in their wake.

I sigh.

Well, that could have gone worse.

Sunshine kisses the side of my neck and snuggles his nose there. "Morning, Sweets."

My heart flutters.

"Morning." I wiggle my butt against his morning wood. "Did you smuggle a banana into bed and didn't tell me about it?"

His throaty morning laughter is music to my ears.

"No?" I faux gasp. "Then who's sneaking bananas into our bed?"

Drawing me firmly against his body, Sunshine groans against my shoulder as his poor cock bucks. Being the sweetest man in existence, he doesn't rut against me. He lets it throb, and when it twitches, I feel every movement, every flex, right against my ass, and damn if that doesn't turn me on. Sex deprivation will do that to a lady.

Sunshine's fingers trail from their home at my breast down to my bare stomach, where he draws circles around my belly button. Goosebumps break out across my body, and I shiver at his touch. "Sweets, we gotta get up," his gravelly morning voice whispers against the back of my head.

"I know." And I do, but it sucks because I fucking adore morning snuggles.

Dropping a quick kiss to my shoulder, Sunshine's the first to roll away. Climbing out of his side of the bed, he rounds to mine, pulls the covers down, and offers me his hand. I clasp it in mine as he draws me from the comfy confines with a dismal groan. This is not how I wanted this morning to go. I wanted pillow talk and relaxation. Maybe a massage. Sunshine gives the best massages. Dark had to ruin our fun. Again.

Together, we enter the bathroom, where he pees with a hard-on, and I turn on the shower to commence our morning ritual. From beneath the bathroom vanity, I collect his toiletries and set the caddy on the floor in the shower stall. Once he's done, Sunshine strips down to nothing, and I get an eyeful of all that is him—big, thick cock, heavy balls, and a tapered waist with those gutters you want to lick whipped cream out of.

Sexy bare feet slap against the tiled floor as he stops right in front of me. Biting my bottom lip, I can't stop looking down at his anatomy because it's been a while since I've gotten such a close-up view. Heat licks up my throat at how fuckin' perfect all of it is.

A throaty laugh rings through the bathroom, and Sunshine hooks a finger under my chin, forcing me to look him in the eye. Not *there*. "I'm gonna shower. You wanna join me?" Those intense grays delve into mine, locking me in place. Beat by beat, they fill with hope. Hope that we'll shower together. That I'll break this invisible barrier between us. I've yet to let him see me as naked as I've seen him. While I love my body, I can't take that step. I can't show him. Not now, and maybe never. Especially not when his son is in the other room with Lily. Not when my panties are soaked, and my pussy aches. Things could happen, and while we skate that line, we never cross it. We're family. We're friends. He's my person and has been since the day he picked me off that floor as a teenager, crying when my mother was dying.

A resigned smile flashes across Sunshine's face before he leans in, presses a long kiss to my forehead, and retreats.

Opening the shower door, he speaks over his shoulder. "I'll be out in a bit, Sweets. You're gonna need to leave unless you wanna watch me play with my cock."

With that, I go, because I can't watch.

In the bedroom, as I get dressed, my mind swirls with vivid images of what he's doing, how he's stroking himself, and wondering if it feels good. Duh. Of course, it does. That's why we masturbate. But still… *how good*?

A long-sleeved sweatshirt and black leggings work for today's lazy fashion as I exit the bedroom and join Dark in the living room while Lily devours a bowl of cereal at the island in the kitchen.

Not wanting to sit beside my ex, I drop into my oversized black chair across from him.

Glaring at me, arms tucked over his chest, he leans forward. "Are you fucking my father?" His words are a harsh, pissed-off whisper, quiet enough that Lily won't overhear.

"No."

His head rears back in surprise. "No?"

"Not that it's any of your business, but no." Not that I haven't thought about it. Obviously. I have two eyes and a fully functioning brain.

"Never?" he presses.

"Never."

Throwing his body back into the couch cushions, Dark's eyes squeeze shut for half a beat before they reopen and search mine. "Thank fuck." He expels a harsh breath.

Yeah.

Sure.

Thank fuck.

This is coming from someone who has a woman he has sex with any time he wants.

Tucking my legs under me, I pull the throw blanket off the back of my chair and drape it over my lap. "Now, what do we need to discuss about this new job of mine?"

Dark produces a manila file and slides it across the coffee table.

For hours, we discuss the details down to the minutia of who, what, when, and where. When Sunshine finishes getting ready for the day, he takes Lily to her bedroom for one-on-one Pops time, to read and play Barbie's, but not before he checks on me. Because let's face it, Dark walking in on this morning will drive an even bigger wedge between them, and there's no telling how much of a dick Dark will act because of it.

So far, he's been okay, even when I force us to stop long enough to make tea and turkey sandwiches in the kitchen. He glares at his father whenever it suits him, but his mouth remains shut on the bedroom matter.

From a mason jar in the fridge, I pour three shot glasses

to the brim with a health tonic I make fresh—lemon juice, ginger, local honey, a dash of orange juice, turmeric, and cayenne. I set the glasses before each guy and leave the last for myself.

"Where's mine?" Lily asks from her stool as she plucks a chip from her plate and devours it.

"Are you sure you want one, Lily Pad?" I check because she's tried the tonic before and nearly threw up. It's potent. Not for the faint of heart.

"Yes. Please." She taps the counter where she wants her shot glass to go.

Dark chuckles, smiling down at his daughter seated beside him. He squeezes her shoulder in pride.

Not wanting to leave her out, I pour my favorite little girl a quarter shot and set it right where she wants.

She's the first to lift it in the air.

Sunshine follows suit, then Dark, and I'm last.

"What should we celebrate?" Lily asks excitedly, the sweetest smile alighting her face.

"To good health?" I shrug.

"To a safe return home," Dark announces, looking straight at me as he clinks his shot glass with Lily's.

"To a safe return home," Sunshine parrots, also staring at me before he taps his tonic to Lily's.

"To a safe return home." Following suit, I clink my glass against everyone's, leaving Dark and Sunshine to finish the honor.

From the opposite side of Lily, Sunshine toasts his son, who returns the gesture with a glare. Together, we down our shots following Lily's joyful, "To a safe return home!"

The juice is smooth and tangy on the way down—a welcome flavor from years of drinking the stuff.

Not everyone's reaction is the same. Lily's face pinches in revulsion, and she forces it down, but not before she gags the tiniest bit. Dark pats her back as he grunts but ingests the tonic like a shot of whiskey with no complaints. Sunshine loves the tonic. He shoots half the glass and savors the flavor before he finishes the second half.

Watching them draws a small smile to my face as the warm fuzziness fill me up inside.

This is my family.

Yes, even Dark.

As the three familial clones finish their lunches, I collect the glasses and place them on the top rack of the dishwasher to run later. Then it's back to work because I have a job to do.

California, here I come.

SEVEN

Setting the stack of empty plates on the galley counter, I prop my hip against it, cross my arms, and wait for Romeo to slide them into the dishwasher.

"Gracias, Hannah." He winks, wearing the kindest eye-crinkling smile, before he jerks his chin over his shoulder toward the gorgeous plate of freshly prepared food—roasted lamb with herb crust on a bed of creamy risotto, a small cotton lined breadbasket with a mini jar of whipped honey-butter, and a slice of decadent triple chocolate cake on the cutest scalloped edged plate. My mouth waters just basking in all its fragrant glory.

"Eat," he orders, sporting a proud grin.

My eyes bulge out of my head. "You want me to eat *that* masterpiece?" I gush, partly because that's how this scenario always plays out, but also because this man *is* a culinary genius.

For two weeks and a few days, we've been pals on the yacht, where I wait on Mr. Cassiano hand and foot—doing his laundry, serving his meals at the outdoor dining table, picking up used condoms off his bedroom floor, ya know, the fun stuff.

I'm one of the three new hires. Romeo's employer goes through *the help* regularly. In other words, he either kills the women, or he sells us. I'm not sure which is more common. I've deduced that the men I deal with daily are his well-paid lackeys, and they're everywhere. Men in suits have him sign paperwork. I've never met a man who signs more paperwork. Then there's the muscle. Your standard buffed-up men wearing shirts three sizes too small, with a permanent scowl etched across their clean-shaven faces. Romeo has been working as a personal chef for Mr. Cassiano for half a decade. They even travel together when Mr. Cassiano has business to attend to elsewhere. I assume this is because he doesn't trust anyone apart from those in his inner circle to handle his food—wise man, given his line of… villainy.

Never one to turn down a Romeo meal, I sit on the stool at the kitchen counter and dive in without shame. Once he's finished loading and running the dishwasher, Romeo leans his lower back against the kitchen cupboards to watch me savor. He even pours me a glass of red, something expensive, far out of the price range we stock at my bar. I'm pretty sure watching me indulge gives Romeo the world's biggest hard-on. That's ego-stroking for you. I'm nothing if not good at my job.

Moaning around a delicious bite, I close my eyes and fake a mini orgasm. Sure, it's good, but this is an act.

Romeo makes a noise, and when I reopen my eyes to make sure he's okay, his tan cheeks are tinged pink.

"This is incredible," I praise, making brief eye contact, the shy, flirty kind, complete with a grin. It never pays to be too forward with men like this, but a well-placed compliment goes miles.

He clears his throat.

I continue to eat and pretend he's not watching.

When I finish my plate, Romeo whisks it away and rinses it in the sink as I start on the cake. Chocolate is my weakness. The longer I've worked here, the more I've consumed world-class chocolate desserts, some of which I can't wait to share with Sugar when I get home. Romeo's an observant man. The first few days I was here, I packed a chocolate croissant for lunch and, the next day, chocolate-covered pretzels as a mid-morning snack. By the third, we had an unforgettable chocolate torte for dinner, and there's been some variation of chocolate every night since.

My assignment wasn't to befriend the chef, but he's been the easiest target, being the friendliest regular on board and closest in age. My employer, Mr. Cassiano, has a type—blondes with big boobs, all barely above legal. I'm a brunette, and according to my paperwork, I'm just over thirty, which is pushing it because, at forty, a decade is a long stretch of convincing. Dark assured me it would work. So far, it has.

So far, this job has been easy… too easy. Too normal. If you consider working for a douchebag millionaire, normal.

I live in a fully furnished single-bedroom apartment, three blocks from the marina, and walk to work most days. Each morning, I don my pressed uniform—a crisp white polo with a blue embroidered logo on the left breast, navy blue trousers, and blue-and-white boat shoes. I haven't worn my hair down in weeks. A slicked-back chignon is required. My makeup is natural, so I look how the media expects us to look when we wake in the morning, but it takes a handful of products and a dewy facial spray to appear that fresh-faced and presentable. Though I do tuck a boob rock or two into my bra before I head out—one can never be too careful. It's no small feat being in the presence of pure evil all day, having to wear a smile, and not take last night's steak knife to stab him in the face—hence the need for crystals. Amethyst and black tourmaline to be exact.

See. Now I'm getting myself worked up over nothing. Well, not nothing. But there is nothing I can do about it right now.

As Gandhi once said, "To lose patience is to lose the battle."

Cutting a too-big bite of cake, I shovel the piece into my mouth and breathe. I focus on the sweetness, the richness of the ganache, and the texture. Re-centering myself, I focus on the good things—like food and new experiences.

There's a charming coffee shop on the boardwalk, a two-minute stroll from the yacht, where I get the best teas and pastries for breakfast, and I'm fed dinner here by Romeo before I head home for the night. Life is simple. Relaxing, even. It's too relaxing given the circumstances.

"How are you going to spend your weekend off?" Romeo asks as he refills my nearly empty glass and pours himself one to finish the bottle.

"I don't know yet. Driving down the coast?" I lie and shove a slice of yummy bread smeared in the world's best butter into my mouth to keep from having to explain.

Romeo hums as if he's mulling over my plans. It's more like he's gauging what I'm doing to report back to his boss. I'm under no illusion where his allegiances lie. Or that he's spying on me just as I'm spying on him. The difference is I know the score. He doesn't. To him, I'm Hannah, a thirty-year-old woman who just left her long-term, cheating boyfriend in Indiana and moved to the coast to start a new life. Dark even registered me for community college in the spring to sell the rouse. Like they care. To them, I'll be dead or sold next week, so the easier they can clean up my disappearance, the better. With no living parents and no siblings, I was a shoo-in for the job.

For the past two weekends, I've played glorified babysitter to naked, barely legal women who drink too much and need help from falling overboard in the middle of the ocean. Oh, and cleaning up the aftermath of the parties that always end in an orgy of rich men, the muscle, and intoxicated women. Not my finest moment, but when you're a mom of two boys who used socks or tissues to clean up their messes, there's not much that fazes me anymore.

What I'm actually doing this weekend is driving up the coast to visit someone. Someone I haven't seen in ages. I'll also talk to Dark. We keep in touch every other day. The closer we get to the main event, the less I'll hear from him. You'd think it would be the opposite, but we have characters to play. He can't worry more about me than I worry about him. We must stay focused.

"What are you doing this weekend?" I ask casually as I sip the rest of my wine and lean back in my chair. I pat my belly for effect.

Seeing I'm finished, Romeo cleans away my dessert dish and my glass when I hand them to him to wash. As he rinses the wares with his back to me, he explains, "There's a farmers' market I visit each month."

"That sounds nice."

"It is perfection. The highest-quality ingredients."

If Sugar said this, I'd ask where the market is and what she planned on buying. In this world, even if I'm curious, I swallow down my questions and smile instead. Asking too many questions and prying can raise suspicions, which we're trying to avoid.

"That's amazing," I say instead, waiting to see if he divulges more.

Romeo dries his hands on a kitchen towel and turns to face me. "How do you feel about filo?"

"For dessert?" I thread my fingers together on the counter and lean forward excitedly. Part an act. Part eager to hear more.

He grins, lopsided and almost shy. "Si."

"Do I get a nibble?"

His surprised laughter booms through the galley. "Oh, yes. A nibble. A whole plate. Whatever you want, *mi amor*." Romeo's head tilts to the side fondly, assessing me as I grin at his flirtation, not exactly welcoming it but not shutting it down either.

"I'll eat anything you make," I reply, leaving any hint of innuendo out of my words. Coming on too strong could backfire, but it doesn't make it any less true. I will eat anything he makes.

"Strawberries?"

Biting my bottom lip, I nod once. "Yes."

"With chocolate?"

My eyes widen, and my mouth waters. He chuckles deep and rumbly, knowing he's got me hook, line, and sinker.

"I'll see what I can find at the market." Romeo winks, and I'm sold. For the next week, I'll get fed by an incredible chef, and then the real fun begins. Finally. I can't wait.

EIGHT

Climbing out of my third Uber of the day, I wave a friendly goodbye to my driver, then heave an irritated sigh as I shut the door and wait for the car to speed off. That's when I return Dark's texts, standing in the middle of a dusty, gravel parking lot as the overhead sun fills me with nature's vitamin D and makes it hard to read whatever mishmash of letters I pound in my haste to tell him to fuck right the hell off.

Thanks to the glare, it takes three tries to fix all the typos.

Me: I don't know how many times I must repeat this. I bought the train ticket! I ordered the Uber using my work phone with my fake name! I entered the building with my bag and turned in my ticket for my phony trip. I changed my clothes in the bathroom, counted to a gazillion, left, and called another Uber using this phone five blocks away.

Him: It was supposed to be six. Six blocks, Kali. Not five.

Me: Maybe it was six.

It was *actually* seven. Fuck him very much, but I'm not telling him that because his instructions are annoyingly detailed. I'm an adult, not a kindergartener. I covered my tracks. To avoid a fight, I did exactly what Dark ordered me to do. Now he's getting on my last nerve for me doing just that. I can't win.

Shoving my phone into the back pocket of my jeans, I ignore the buzzing against my ass and enter the roadside restaurant out in the middle of no-fucking-where. From the outside, the western-styled bar and grill looks like a dilapidated shithole. The inside feels like home.

A portly, snaggle-toothed waitress carrying an armful of plastic menus lumbers to the front door to greet me. She's downright adorable as she aggressively points to the rear of the bar and grins. "Girl, git your bony ass where it belongs."

Throwing my head back, a laugh rips out of my throat. "It's nice to see you, too, Marge." I pat her shoulder as I do just that—get my bony ass where it belongs. Not that I think I have a bony behind. My ass is shapely. Maybe not bootylicious, but there's a slope—a curve. Not all of us can be graced with two dump trucks attached to our rears like dear ole Marge.

Tucked in a back corner, two dark heads sit around a table. Giddiness ignites in my veins as I approach.

I tussle the one with the fullest head of hair.

"Hey, Mom," he greets, looking up at me from his seat as his brother Tarek snickers and two-finger waves—his typical male greeting.

"Hey, back. Long time no see, stranger." I smooch his upturned forehead. "Wasn't sure if you were gonna show today." Wanting to remain close to him, I pull out the well-worn chair next to my son and claim it for myself.

Marge rushes in before we get a chance to chat, drops plastic menus on the table in front of each of my boys, and arches a gray, brushy brow in my direction. "The uzhe?"

"Has the menu changed?" I tease, already knowing the answer.

She flips me off.

I smile like a movie star.

"The uzhe, it is," she crows, then turns her attention to my sons when she says, "You two look just like your daddy and grandpa." She whistles as if they're the hottest men she's ever laid eyes on. Around these parts, that's partly true. This dot on a map is more than a bar and grill. It's a safe space for bikers. The number of leather-clad, weapon-toting men that frequent this place is the only reason it's stayed afloat all these years. They even have a backroom for meetings—or church, if you're hip with the motorcycle club lingo.

That sounded lame, didn't it?

Hip with the lingo.

Shoot me now.

Tarek grins and puffs up his chest at her compliment, more for Marge's benefit than his. He's a good kid.

Fog remains stoic, showing no emotion.

I don't expect anything different.

Being reminded he looks anything like his father is never… good. Fog took Dark's cheating the hardest. Probably harder than me, if that's possible. He idolized his father down to his clothes, his favorite music, and even the movies he watched. Unlike his brother, Fog wanted to be a Sacred Sinner since he started walking. The aftermath of Dark's deception destroyed their relationship like a land mine neither of them could avoid. There is a thin line between love and hate, and their line is damn near invisible. For years,

Dark has tried to mend fences. I know he has. But I'm sure you can guess how that's gone.

Marge reads the room like the smart cookie she is and vanishes to give the boys a chance to pick their lunch.

Elbows perched on the table edge, head hanging low, fingers shoved through his hair, Fog sits in despair like Fog always does, being the most sensitive, introspective of my kids. He's also the biggest at well over six foot three and, if I had to put a number on it, in the range of three hundred pounds, or so his size 2XL shirts would indicate.

Drumming his fingers on the table's edge, Tarek grins at me as if his brother isn't having a crisis. "Sooo…" he drawls. "I hear you only went five blocks."

This little shithead.

"You talked to Dad," I guess as the hairs on the back of my arms stand on end, sending a chill down my spine.

"Yeah. He talked to Dad," a gruff voice speaks from behind me.

I freeze.

Smoother than silk, the Devil himself slides the chair out beside me, across from Fog, and bumps his foot against mine as it settles under the table.

I forget to breathe.

Fog squeezes my knee beneath the table in tune with my internal freakout.

I dislodge a stuttering breath.

Dark reaches out to tuck a strand of hair around the shell of my ear like it's a normal day in some new reality I'm unaware of.

My heart punches my sternum like we're in a heavy-weight boxing match. My muscles seize, turning my frame into an ironing board, as I wait for him to extract his *every-*

thing from my bubble. Once his featherlight touch clears my earlobe, it trails lower to drag across my neck. Somebody kill me now, pinch me, or whatever works. I don't like this dream.

Not down with his father's games, Fog glares at Dark as his hand on my knee tightens. I cuff my palm over his to communicate all is well. That I'm okay. Sure, I'm a little surprised. I didn't expect Dark to show up. You'd think I'd have noticed his bike in the parking lot. When I arrived, I'd seen Tarek's sleek black Harley and Fog's red, flaming devil. Then again, by the looks of Dark, he's in undercover mode —an expensive black suit and a crisp white shirt unbuttoned at the throat where that stupidly attractive tattoo lives. No tie or pocket square. Simple yet sexy. It's a stark contrast compared to my leather-cut, t-shirt, and jeans-wearing sons.

"I take it you didn't ride in?" I force out when my ex finally gives me space.

"Nope. The black Mercedes is mine for now." Dark relaxes in his chair.

I hum in response, not knowing what else to say. I didn't see the car when I arrived. Then again, he could have arrived after me and snuck in. Or he could be parked out back. Not that it matters.

Marge takes this opportunity to integrate herself back into our family reunion. Looking at Dark, she wipes the back of her hand across her forehead like she might faint. Then the wicked woman leans down and whispers toward me, but loud enough that the entire table can hear, "Is it just me, or has he gotten sexier?" She fans her face as her cheeks burn bright red.

Tarek snickers.

The jerk himself beams like she handed him a trophy

and takes it a step further when he blows the woman a kiss. This might very well be the end of poor Marge, as she almost swoons right off her feet. Before she collapses, I reach out and grip her forearm to keep her upright. Her gaze locked on my ex, Marge blinks a handful of times before she clears her throat and pats the top of my hand, which remains gently cuffed around her arm. When I'm convinced she won't keel over, I let go.

Marge's gaze swings from Dark to me. "Thank ya, darlin'." She pats my shoulder. "I'm gonna get ya an extra slice of pie for that."

I open my mouth to tell her it's unnecessary. Trust me, I understand the effects Dark has on women, and that's why he does what he does for the club. Her matronly stare cuts me off before I can make a peep. "Let's hope it'll give ya a bigger hiney." Marge flashes me a mischievous wink. Then she's gone, lumbering away as if she didn't just insult my ass.

Tarek cackles.

Rubbing my temple with my middle finger, I covertly flip him the bird.

Dark smirks but doesn't let the teasing insult go when he calls to Marge's retreating form loud enough for the entire restaurant to hear, "Kali's ass is perfect the way it is."

The handful of men at the bar hoot like a cluster of buffoons.

Pinching the bridge of my nose, I quell the urge to kick Dark in the shin for opening his big mouth. Was that necessary? I think not. Nobody needs to come to the defense of my ass, except me. I am perfectly capable of defending myself.

"Right answer, lover boy," Marge replies. "Your uzhe is

comin' right up. But I'm tellin' Hank to add extra onions." The woman whistles a merry tune all the way to the kitchen.

Dark drags a hand down his face and groans.

"It's gonna be the whole plate." I press my lips together to keep from bursting into maniacal laughter.

"I know." Dark's chin hits his chest in defeat.

"You shouldn't have almost given her a heart attack."

He snorts. "I was bein' nice."

Sure, he was.

"You're playin' with fire."

My ex glances up and bats his pretty lashes at me. "I'm only playin' with fire when I'm with you, babe."

Not at all impressed, I roll my eyes.

"Shut the fuck up." Fog points at his father. "I didn't agree to be here so you could talk to Mom like that."

Not wanting to make things worse, Dark raises both hands in mock surrender. "It was a joke."

"No, it wasn't." Fog grips the table's edge like he's about to come across it any second. The vein in his neck throbs as he clenches his jaw so hard I'm afraid he'll crack a tooth.

Worried about my son, I grasp his knee under the table this time. My hand doesn't cover much, but it conveys enough. "It's okay, sweetheart. I'm good." I double-squeeze to communicate I'm not lying. Because I'm not. I *am* okay.

Fog's glare finally breaks from Dark and swings to me, where it softens. "He's a fuckin' dick."

"I know." My voice is a mere whisper.

"This is such a fun family outing. We should do this more often," Tarek deadpans without an ounce of mirth. Though, I see the glint of smartassery in his eyes.

Head shaking as if he doesn't know whether to punch his brother or let shit go, Fog's lip kicks up in the corner in a microscopic grin. It's gone in a flash, but the tension at the table disappears, which gives me a chance to soak in the presence of my boys as they finally scan their menus. It's been months since I've seen either of them in person. FaceTime is great, but nothing beats ruffling their hair or watching them smile in person. Marge was spot-on when she said they resemble their father and Sunshine, and it goes beyond the physical. It's even in the way they move—like predators, graceful with purpose. The simple act of flipping over their menus is familiar. It's nice. This is nice. I'm glad they came today.

Marge returns with a round of water and takes the boys' orders and menus. She doesn't write any of it down. Not even Tarek's list of burger additions—he has a thing for mozzarella sticks on burgers, and not in replacement of the cheese, in addition to it. Don't ask. It's Sunshine's doing—a diner experience when Tarek was little. Fog's a different story. He's simple. When he says, "Give me the best thing you got," he means it.

"You sure?" Marge tucks the menus under her arm.

"Yes, ma'am," Fog replies with a definitive nod.

Grinning at his politeness, Marge pats my kid on the shoulder. Looks like he's earned himself an extra slice of pie, too. People Marge likes are treated like royalty by her and her husband Hank. If royalty consists of extra homemade dessert. To me, that feels a whole lot like royalty. The people who piss them off get onions. Don't ask me why it's onions. I have no idea and never had the heart to ask.

Since the first time I met Marge, over two decades ago, on a visit to one of the California Chapters, I've adored her. She was just as sassy back then as she is now, but she got around better. Age will do that to ya. Being on your feet running this place six days a week will also do that to ya.

Dark sips his water. "Five blocks, huh?" He speaks against the edge of his glass before he takes a bigger drink.

Looks like we're still stuck on my Uber from the station. Why are we back to this conversation? I thought the case was closed.

"It was seven." I spill the truth because enough is enough. What is it with these men?

"Told you." Tarek puts his hand out, rocking an *I-win, pay-up-sucker* smile.

Grumbling good-natured expletives under his breath, Dark yanks his wallet from the inside pocket of his suit jacket. It's full of big bills as he rifles through them and slaps a crisp fifty into our son's open palm.

Fog stretches his tattooed hand across the table, mimicking his brother's pose. Dark doesn't hesitate to slap a fifty there, too. If Mr. Moneybags wants to spread the wealth, I'd happily take some of that off his hands. But I know it's not his money. It's the clubs. He's playing his part of the rich man, ready to buy high-dollar pussy at an illegal auction. Dark's acting skills are immaculate, which is why being married to him was scary at times. Worrying about what was real and what might be fake messed with my head when we were younger. Especially when he was gone for weeks, sometimes months at a time, and he couldn't tell where he'd gone, what he'd done, or why they needed him there. Club business stays club business. Thankfully, as the boys grew older, he took fewer assignments that kept him away from us for longer than a week or two. Until Abby and we all know how that went.

"So, we're betting on Mom now, are we?" I gesture to the money they're stowing in their respective wallets.

Tarek sits forward to slide his wallet back into his rear pocket. "Dad's been blowing up my phone—"

"Tarek," Dark hisses, slapping his palm on the tabletop.

"What?" Resettling in his seat, our son shrugs a single shoulder up and down. "It's true."

Squeezing his eyes shut as if he wants nothing to do with this conversation, Dark shrinks in his chair and crosses both arms over his big chest. Once again, his foot knocks into mine under the table before it starts to bounce. My heart jolts at the accidental contact, and I turn my body away to keep him from doing it again.

Ignoring his father's reaction, Tarek keeps talking. "Dad's been worried about you."

"Okay?" That's nothing new.

"You need to check your apartment."

Ah. Shit. Here we go.

"Christ," Dark bites off, shaking his head in frustration.

"Why?" I look between them for answers.

Tarek's the first to fill in the blanks. "Dad had cameras installed."

He what? *What?*

Hating where this is headed, I massage the frown lines between my brows as they begin to ache. "He… I don't understand."

Shifting in his chair, Dark stares at me straight-on. "We agreed you need to be safe."

Fog nods as if he concurs with his father's sentiment, which shocks the hell out of me. Them on the same side of anything doesn't compute.

"I agreed to no such thing," Tarek chimes in. "Invading

Mom's privacy without her knowledge is bullshit, and you both know it. Pops agreed."

Great. Sunshine's involved, too. It's a family affair.

The other two males at the table remain quiet, and I feel like I've been sucker punched. I have cameras in my apartment. Why would they need to be inside my apartment, and why wouldn't he have asked before installing them? Inside my apartment is the safest place I can be on this assignment. It's in a gated complex with eight units. It's small. It's secure. That was the point of me moving there.

An awkward silence descends.

Tarek relaxes back in his chair as if his conscience is now clear.

Blowing out a breath, I try to navigate this. "Sooo," I drawl. "I came up here on my only weekend off to see my sons, and when I get back to my apartment, I have to search for cameras. What the hell, guys?"

My ex lifts his glass and takes a long sip of water. I watch his throat work as he swallows. "You're ours to protect."

That's his explanation. Really?

"Wrong. I protect myself." I point to my chest for emphasis. "*Who* has access to my apartment cameras?"

"Dad," Tarek answers, staring pointedly at his father as if waiting for him to deny it. But he does no such thing.

"Dark. What the fuck? *You* asked me to be a part of this. I have followed every single order you have given me. I have built a friendly relationship with—" I stop talking and look around as if there are cameras here with microphones, listening to our conversation, even though I know that's impossible. Marge chases out the riffraff, and Hank is a former biker, who I'm pretty sure sweeps for bugs daily to keep their clientele safe. Leaning forward so far that my breasts press against the table's edge, I gesture to our sons with a flick of my chin. "Am I even allowed to speak about this in mixed company?"

My ex nods. "Yes. They've been briefed."

This motherfucker.

"Why were our sons briefed, Dark?" Reaching inside my front pocket, I extract a small, tumbled obsidian crystal and slam it down on the table in front of him because he's going to need it—for protection from me. I'm gonna murder him for real this time. It's a miracle it doesn't shatter under the force of my rage.

The jerk stares at the small stone with wide, expressive gray eyes, then at me. For a suspended moment, I think he's going to do or say something, but then he blinks, and the cool mask of indifference descends, locking into place. One that can't be penetrated because he no longer cares to care. He's Dark, the businessman. Dark, the biker. He doesn't have feelings. He's a big, bad man.

Fuck him.

"Because I wanted them to be." My ex shrugs as if this isn't a big deal, but it's an enormous deal to me.

"Dark," I whisper-hiss.

"Yes?" he replies in his uppity, posh tone that makes my skin crawl.

"I told you," Tarek announces as if he's telling his father and brother they've done fucked up. Because they have.

But this Dark doesn't care.

This Dark is a person I hate. Not the fake hate created from a broken heart and shattered dreams. The real kind, where you can't even look at the asshole any longer. Because I know if I do, I'll get up and leave and never turn back. I'll ruin any chance I have of catching up with my boys. They are what I came here for. Not him. He wasn't even supposed to be here.

Needing space, I remove myself from the table to use the ladies' room. I take too much time washing my hands and staring at myself in the mirror for no reason other than to bide my time in hopes Marge will bring our food before I return.

Wanting to look nice for Tarek and Fog, I wore makeup today—smokey eyes and blood-red lips. I also put effort into my outfit since I haven't been able to since the start of my *job*—dark skinny jeans, a charcoal t-shirt with an Edgar Allen Poe quote on it, and black Chucks. Is it wildly fashionable? No. It's comfortable and fitting for a biker bar.

The door to the restroom opens. Marge comes in with a concerned expression etched across her face. "What happened?"

Heaving a sigh, I lean my hip against the sink. "My ex is a dick."

"Oh, honey, we know." She waves the knowledge off. "We all know. Damn, fine man, fucked up and lost a damn fine woman. Even if I hadn't asked Hank to give him onions, he would have done it on principle alone." Sprier than she's been all day, Marge swoops in and hugs me up tight, much like I suspect a grandma would, had I ever known mine. Not realizing how much I needed this, I return the embrace with just as much strength, and Marge grunts. "Don't break these bones now."

Inhaling her familiar mixture of beer, cheap perfume, and fried food scent, I chuckle. "I won't."

Marge is the first to pull away but doesn't go far when she thumbs toward the closed door. "I made a call. Figured you might need a little distraction."

"Marge. What did you do?"

"I said I made a call." The wicked woman smiles like she ate the canary and leaves me standing in the bathroom, watching the door suction itself closed with the nosiest hiss.

Then I hear a memorable voice before I see her.

The bathroom door slowly opens, and a blue-haired sprite of a woman walks in.

"Pixie!" I rush one of my oldest friends and hug her up, much like Marge did with me.

Her small arms wrap around my center as she giggles like a tinkly fairy at my enthusiasm. "Hey, Kali."

Once I've gotten my fill, I pull back and give her a solid once-over. It's been years since I last saw her in person. "You look amazing," I gush, gesturing toward the bright tattoos flowing up both arms, now traveling onto her throat.

Not one to take compliments well, the shy woman blushes a thousand shades of crimson and combs a shaky hand through her hair. "Thanks. I think." Unable to look at me, she stares at the white bathroom wall until her discomfort fizzles away.

There's a quiet knock on the bathroom door.

"Kali. Marge said to get your…" The male clears his throat uncomfortably, like he can't say the words.

"My bony ass out there?" I answer for him as a giant smile spreads across my face.

The door opens, revealing the smallest gap, and Axel, Pixie's old man, peeks through it. "Care to join us?"

Leading the way, my friend snatches my hand. Ever the gentleman, Axel opens the door for us to pass and rejoin my family—where two more chairs have been set for our guests, and plates of steaming food fill every inch of the tabletop. We pack in like sardines, and I've never been more grateful for the distraction in my life. Despite the solid, three-inch pile of onions on top of Dark's chili cheese fries, he had better cough up a big tip for Marge. This spread is fantastic.

On a plate bigger than my head, my breaded chicken salad with homemade croutons and ranch is a sight for sore eyes. Famished, I dive in as Tarek scoops his dad's onions off his plate onto his own. Even Pixie and Axel have piping hot breakfast platters ready to devour. The food soothes me. So many nights, we ended up here, laughing and carrying on with our friends, much like this. Those were simpler times when Pixie lived here with her family. Before she and Axel moved across the country to the Sacred Sinner's Mother Chapter, where Pixie owns an all-female tattoo shop. It's wild to think we spent many nights here talking about her dream of doing just that.

Throughout lunch, Dark carefully shovels the messiest of fries into his mouth with a fork and fingers the obsidian rock beside his plate. Now and again, as he chats with Axel, he'll look over, smile, and resume whatever they're talking about.

Fog plucks a crouton from my plate and crunches down. I nudge the butthead's foot under the table, and my son genuinely smiles at me for the first time since I got here, releasing a tightness in my chest I didn't know was there. For the first time all day, I breathe easier in the company of those I love the most, minus Sunshine and Lily.

When Dark and Axel finish their meals first, they leave to throw darts at the far side of the bar beside the red-felted pool tables with beer logo lights hanging above them. Not long after, our sons join them, but not before Fog and Tarek tidy up their empty plates and kiss my cheek. Marge sneaks in once they've left and steals Dark's chair. Probably in hopes she can smell him. I can't say I blame her. He does smell amazing, and she has always had a crush on him and Sunshine.

"You're on a job?" Pix asks once the men are far from earshot.

I nod, and she leaves it at that, knowing I can't divulge more, even though I'd love to.

Placing both palms on the tabletop, Marge leans in conspiratorially. "What is going on with you two?" Her gaze swaps from our table to Dark and the guys.

"With Dark?" I ask to be sure.

Her nod confirms my question.

"We're on the same assignment." I pluck a lonesome crouton from the corner of my half-full plate and pop it into my mouth.

"Ah. Makes sense. He called yesterday to make sure I only let our regulars in today and called again this morning to double-check."

"He's protective of me."

"Because he loves you."

"In his own way. Yes," I agree and turn toward Pixie to change the subject. "How's the shop?"

"It's great. How's the tattoo?"

Alone in our restaurant area, I get out of my seat and pull up my shirt to the edge of my bra, exposing part of my back and my stomach. I do a complete turn.

Having never seen this side of me before, Marge's mouth opens and closes like a fish.

Sliding from her seat onto mine, Pix examines her masterpiece with scrutiny only an artist would. She hums thoughtfully as I turn slowly, allowing her to see it for the first time in years.

"This is some of my best work," she whispers, more to herself than us. "It's aged just how I thought it would."

She's right. It has.

From my ribs down to my hips, wrapping around both sides and up my entire back, is the colorful story of me—entangled in an intricate garden of life.

In the center of my stomach, where I bore my sons, is my favorite scene—a skull lying in a bed of roses with two ravens standing upon its head, facing one another. Between their beaks is a real heart, like the one beating in our chests. Blood drips from the organ down the front of the skull into the flower bed below, right above my womb. To some, it may look creepy. To me, it's symbolic—bleeding lifeblood into our children. The ravens are a representation of Dark and me. Two becoming one. Vines and flowers wrap from there, up my sides, onto my back, where a lily blooms, and at the top of my shoulder, there's a sun, and with its brilliant light, it feeds the flowers below. Sunshine.

Everyone is here, inked into flesh. Nobody would guess I had a tattoo covering this much of my body. But that's the point, isn't it? With clothes on, I can look normal if I want to, whatever that means. With them off, the deepest parts of me are revealed.

Squinting, Marge points to something on my side. "Is that a crystal frog sitting on a leaf?"

Pix turns me to give Marge a better view. "It sure is."

"He's cute," she says.

"Thanks." I chuckle, enjoying Marge's awe far too much.

Did you know, in Egyptian mythology, frogs represent fertility and new life? When I was homeschooled, Mom had an entire section on amphibians in the Mythos. Frogs and toads hold a lot of weight in many ancient cultures. As a kid, I was obsessed with them.

"How long did all that take?" Marge gestures toward all of me.

"Twelve sessions, I think," Pix answers. "That's somewhere between fifty to seventy-five hours."

Leaning back in her chair and crossing both arms under her ample breasts, Marge sniffs. "And men think women are weak."

"Women do sit better for tattoos. Though I've done most of Dark's ink, and he's taken it well," Pixie explains.

"Even the throat?" Marge touches her neck.

Pix nods. "Yep. Even the throat."

"Shee-it," Marge whistles, impressed. That makes two of us. I was with him when he got the tattoo—one session and one touch-up a month later, that's all it took.

"Don't let him fool ya, Marge. Dark whined for three days when his throat swelled, and he had trouble sleeping." He was miserable, hating life. We went through a dozen ice packs, and he refused to shower in anything other than water cold enough to shrivel his balls.

"That shouldn't make me feel better, but it does." The wicked woman smiles.

Once Pixie's gone over every inch of my tattoo, I drop my shirt back into place. Just as I do, Fog appears at our table. "Can I talk to you about something?" He touches my arm and jerks his chin toward the front door. I guess we need to talk outside.

Leaving the ladies to chat, I trail my son out the front. He doesn't stop there but walks around the side of the building to the back, where he leans against the dilapidated siding beside a row of dumpsters, and I post in front of him.

"What's up, kiddo?" I ask.

Fidgeting, refusing to make eye contact, Fog looks up to the sky. "What I'm about to tell you, Tarek already knows."

That sounds… ominous.

"Okayyy?" I drawl.

"You can't tell Dad."

Oh, boy. This doesn't sound promising.

"Okay. I won't," I vow and cross my heart so he knows I'm serious. I wouldn't ever betray his trust.

Puffing up his shoulders like he's pumping himself up to say whatever he brought me out here to say, Fog tugs at the edges of his cut. "Tarek said I need to stop lying."

"Lying about what, exactly?"

My son expels a harsh breath and tips his head down to stare at the gravel beneath our feet, still refusing to make eye contact. He kicks a bigger rock with the toe of his boot, and it flies under one of the dumpsters. "I know this isn't the best time." He chews on his bottom lip.

"It's always a good time to talk to your mother." I speak softly, hoping to coax this kid out of his shell.

"What if I said I… Fuck…" Kicking another rock, Fog massages the nap of his neck. "What if I… said I… had a… partner?" He forces the words out as if they are scary to say.

"I'd ask if it was serious and when I could meet them?" I tread lightly because this seems to be a big deal.

Still staring at the ground like it's the most fascinating thing, he bobs his head along with my words. "What if it wasn't a…" he trails off, unable to form the words.

A ball of excitement ignites in my belly like a basket of caffeinated frogs.

"Oh. *Ohhhh…*" I clap loudly and bounce on the balls of my feet. This is it. It's finally happening!

Fog looks up at me with the widest, most expressive eyes. "What are you doing, Mom?"

"You're gonna say it," I cheer, thrusting a hand in the air.

My son frowns, the lines in his forehead stressing as he looks at me as if I've been possessed. "I'm gonna say what?"

"Is this when you come out of the closet?" I squeak.

"What?"

"Are you dating a man?" The words rush out because it's happening! It's finally happening!

Please be brave. Please be brave. You can do this.

"Am I…" Fog chokes on his words. "Am I…"

"Dating a man?" I urge, far less chill than I planned to be when the day came.

"Mom."

"Is that a yes?" My feet can't stop moving as I wiggle in place.

My son's frown deepens to the point if anyone sees us, they fear for my life, but I'm not worried. He's not mad. He's struggling. "Mom, why are you dancing?"

Unable to stop, I wiggle, wiggle, wiggle in the rocks, creating a small crater with my feet. "Because… I'm excited! Are you dating a man?" I sound hopeful, too hopeful.

"Mom, you're freakin' me out."

"Because you're ready to tell me you're gay?"

You've got this. You've got it, Fog. Just say the words. Say the damn words!

"Mom."

"What?" I jam an eager hand into my pocket to pull out the red tiger's eye crystal and offer it to my son—for courage.

With a shake of his head and the cutest of crooked grins, he places his palm out, face up. I drop the crystal right onto his heartline, and he crushes his fist around it like it's a lifeline as he breathes in deep, expanding his chest. Tears well in his eyes as he swallows thickly. Then, the moment happens. The sky opens, and the world aligns, and finally, fucking finally, my son utters the words I've been waiting on forever. "Yes. I'm dating a man."

Slamming my body into Fog's with more force than I intend, he crashes into the back of the building as I wrap him into the biggest mama bear hug. Laughing with tears trickling down his cheeks, he returns the embrace and encases me in his cushy softness. I stuff my nose between his pecs and breathe in the fresh scent of mint and man.

"I'm so proud of you," I speak to his heart. To his brave soul.

"Thanks, Mom." He chuckles wetly and kisses the top of my head.

"So. So. Proud!" I crow into the cotton of his shirt.

Resting my cheek against his sternum, arms locked around his middle, I listen to the wild beat of Fog's heart as his chest expands with deep, emotional breaths. Imbuing all my love through our connection, I wait for him to soak in the realness of the moment and relax. Inside my head, I whisper encouragement and mantras of strength handed down to me from my mother—*Om Gam Ganapataye Namaha*. Eventually, a quiet calm descends, his tense muscles uncoil, and his heart rate returns to normal. Only then do I break our embrace and step back far enough to look him in the eye but close enough to reach up and thumb away the wetness cascading down his cheek.

"You already knew, huh?" The slightest grin ticks up at the corner of Fog's mouth.

"Of course I did. For many years." I'm a mother. We notice things.

He squeezes his fist around the crystal still in his hand. "And you just waited?" He sounds offended.

"Yes." I'd wait forever if I had to. That's what mothers do.

"Why? This would have been a lot easier if you'd have told me you knew."

"It's not my place to tell you who you are. You'd tell me whenever you were ready."

"I've been stressing over this for years."

I shrug. "Well, no more stressing."

"That's not so easy," Fog groans. "I'm a biker. Liking dick isn't widely supported."

This is true, but the Sacred Sinners aren't like other clubs. Sure, you have your assholes, but a gay couple—Bear and Ghost, run the Texas chapter, and nobody gives a damn.

"If they have a problem with it, they have Dad, Pops, and Tarek to deal with. And me. I'm scariest of them all." I throw my hands out to show how scary I can be, and I twist my face into something terrifying. Sort of.

The scariness isn't effective when my son chuckles. It's low and shakes his entire frame. I try not to take offense. "That's true."

"Which part?"

"That you're the scariest." Shaking his head, Fog smiles at my level of ridiculousness. He knows I'm right.

"See. I got your back, and… Dad and Pops already know, so you might as well tell them. They've been waiting, too."

Fog blinks as if he didn't expect me to say that. "*Dad* knows? *Pops* knows?"

"Duh." Listen, as much as I love my son and would have waited until the end of time for him to tell me he was into dudes, he wasn't exactly covert when he made off-handed comments about attractive actors and the number of men's magazines with built, older men I found in his room was enough to confirm any suspicion. Those mixed with his lack of dating females, and I easily put two and two together.

"And Dad doesn't care?" Fog asks as if that's news to him.

"Why would he care unless the guy you're dating is a douchebag?"

"Because he's Dad."

"Exactly. He's Dad. Raised by Pops, one of the most open-minded men I've ever met." There's not a single bigoted bone in either of their bodies. Just because Fog and Dark haven't been on the best of terms doesn't mean he's some asshole father who would hate or disown his kid for loving whoever he loved. If Fog suddenly said he was into imaginary rainbow fairies and needed to catch them in a magical net made of silk, they'd weave the net themselves and help him catch a fairy. No questions asked. That's what you do for family.

Fog rolls the tiger's eye between his thick fingers. "Tarek warned me."

"Warned you how?"

"That I was being an idiot."

Then Tarek was right.

"Because you were worried?" I ask to be sure. "Wait. Is this why you haven't been texting me back lately?"

Looking everywhere but me, Fog replies a quiet, "Yes."

This kid. Ugh. Every call and text has been met with one or two-word responses. Never full sentences. It's been going on for months. I asked Tarek about it. He said Fog was busy. That he'd get back to me soon. I chalked it up to young adulthood. Not everyone wants to chat with their mom once they're grown. They're too cool for that. It happens. Eventually, most outgrow that phase. Or so I hear.

Crowding him with my much smaller body, I pop my kid upside his skull. "Calvin Fog, don't do that shit again," I scold.

My son snickers and rubs the side of his head. "I won't." He smiles down at me as if he finds me cute. To him, I probably am. That's what happens when you have boys who are already taller than you before they hit high school.

"I mean it." I wag my finger at him like only moms can. "We're a family. We get through things together." Finished getting my point across, I put my finger weapon away. "Now, do you have a picture of your boyfriend? Does Tarek like him? Is he another Sacred Sinner? Does he know your mom is a little crazy?" I rattle off, sounding far more like Cell than I care to admit.

Pulling out his phone from his front pants pocket, Fog opens it with a swipe. And there he is… My son's boyfriend is on the screen when he holds it out for me.

Wow. Okay. That's not what I was expecting. Perhaps a cute twink. Someone younger.

"He's older than you," I observe, noting the lines accentuating his eyes and bracketing his lips as he smiles. Attractive, but older, much older. Dark's gonna murder him.

"He is," Fog confirms with an adorable, shy grin, swiping to show me another picture and then another of his boyfriend. He has good taste, I'll give him that.

When he lands on a shirtless photo, I grow slightly uncomfortable. "Don't tell your father," I whisper-hiss, knowing Dark will want to murder this guy. A pocket-sized, college-age boy. Perfect. This guy… Correction…. This *man…* is much older and just as big as Fog, and we've already established how large my son is.

Frowning down at me, Fog appears confused. "Don't tell Dad what?"

"Any of this." I gesture to his phone and the photo of his man wearing a club vest.

"But you said he already knows."

"He does. Unofficially. If you tell him, he's gonna ask the same questions, and he's gonna hate you're dating a man *that* age."

As much as I love my son and am overjoyed he's finally comfortable being himself, dating someone much older scares me—for his sake, not mine. They are decades apart. He's barely out of high school compared to a man who has tons of life experience.

"I'm an adult," he argues, not at all on board with my concern.

Not wanting to ruffle his feathers any further, I gently touch my kid's arm to calm him. "You're still his son," I speak softly.

Whatever fight is brewing in Fog deflates the second he realizes I'm on his side. Always. No matter what. If he's happy, I'm happy.

"Do you really think this is gonna be a problem?"

"With Dad? Probably. He's protective of everyone in our family. And if he knows him, that's gonna be worse."

"Dad does know him."

"Of course he does." I massage the bridge of my nose. "What's his name?"

"Lace."

Hmmm… Lace. I've heard that name before, but I can't place where.

"You guys out here?" Tarek calls, rounding the corner to join us—the heels of his boots crunching through the gravel.

Tarek takes one look at us, at Fog's phone, and presses his lips together like he's trying hard not to laugh.

"I know," I announce to my eldest. "But Dad's gonna be pissed when he finds out who he's dating."

"Lace is a good dude," Tarek defends, surprising the heck out of me.

Is it just me, or does today keep getting weirder and weirder? I came here for lunch and to catch up with my sons, only to see Dark, visit with Pixie, and now this. Not that I'm complaining. I'm happy for Fog, and Dark hasn't pissed me off too much.

Turning to Tarek, I put my hand on my hip. "So. Spill."

"Spill what?" He runs a hand through his hair.

"If Fog's sharing big news, I'm sure you have something to share." I arch my brow and wait for him to come clean.

"Like what?" Tarek looks genuinely baffled.

"I don't know. That's what I'm trying to figure out. Fog wouldn't randomly come out of the closet. It doesn't fit his personality. Why today? Why now?"

They share a look.

Then, it dawns on me like a light switch being flipped on.

The assignment.

The risk.

The need to protect me.

"You told me because of the assignment," I address my youngest.

Fog shrugs up one of his big shoulders and drops it hard. Yep. Thought so. That's confirmation enough. When I run jobs for the club, the details are secure. Nobody but me, Cell, sometimes Sunshine, and on occasion, Dark knows. But this one, Dark got permission to brief them. No wonder they're acting strange, even Dark, with him placing the cameras and Tarek calling him out for it. Then Fog's support of wanting to keep me safe despite the problems with his father. They're concerned. They don't know what I've done for the club. How deep I've gone. All they know is I'm their mom, who runs intel. They don't know about all the other stuff.

Awe. My kids love me—so much that Fog came out just in case something happened, he wouldn't leave anything unsaid.

I dramatically clutch my chest. "You two are the cutest."

Tarek rolls his eyes until all I see are the whites. "Go inside, Mom."

I turn to Fog and pat his chest. "I'm proud of you and always will be. Tell Dad, don't tell Dad, that's up to you. I've got your back either way." Finishing the conversation, I kiss both of my sons on their cheeks before I leave them to figure out their plans and make my way back inside, where my ex awaits me right inside the door.

"Here." He hands me his phone.

On the screen is my favorite little girl. "Kali!" Lily screeches, waving at me wildly from what looks to be her bedroom at home. Dark painted the walls black six months ago. I don't know a little girl who loves black as much as her.

Snickering at her outburst, I take the phone to the unused waiting area, dust off the bench, and sit down. The old plastic creaks under my weight as the rows of silver duct tape try to keep the ancient pad together. "How are you?"

For what feels like hours but is only like ten minutes, Lily rambles nonstop. I listen as Dark leans against the wall a few feet away, eavesdropping on us. Not that I mind. She is his daughter.

When Tarek and Fog return, they say hello to their sister before Fog gives me a signal that I think means he's about to spill the truth to Dark. When Tarek slaps his father on the back, and they approach the bar for a round of beers, I know they're doing just that.

Pixie and Marge eventually find me in the waiting area and join the fun. They get to experience all of Lily's adorableness up close and personal. When Marge pipes in to ask Lily questions about herself, the little girl beams, and I hand over Dark's phone for them to carry on. Having no kids, therefore no grandkids of her own, Marge soaks up her time with Lily like she's one of the family. I guess she is, in a way.

"How long are you here for?" I ask Pixie as Marge discusses cartoons, and Lily explains why *Coraline* is the best movie ever made.

"A few more days. I'm here to tattoo my brother Coal. Then, who knows what? We're supposed to be on lockdown since we're at war, but Big gave us the okay to visit since it's family."

"Who are you staying with?"

"Coal. He has an extra apartment for friends and family to stay in when they visit. Thankfully, it's on the other side of his house," Pix says, sounding relieved.

"So you don't run into his flavor of the week?" I guess, grinning as I recall a laundry list of sordid Coal stories I've heard over the years.

"Exactly." Pix nods as she pulls a face. "I thought he'd stop man-whoring by now, but he's worse now than the last time you probably saw him."

Humming, I tap my lips and reflect on my last run-in with Pixie's infamous sex-fiend brother. "The last time I saw

Coal, he had two girls on his arm and one sucking his dick at a pool party." That was a wild night. Drunk on cheap wine, Dark and I had sex in the pool house on top of an old dryer.

Slapping her leg, Pixie's tinkly laugh fills the air. "Well, I suppose not much has changed then."

"No. I suppose not," I return with a chuckle.

We catch up on old times until Lily finally lets Marge go, and Dark returns from the bar with our sons to retrieve his phone. He jerks his chin at me as if he'd like to speak privately. Making eye contact, I nod and get up from the bench to follow him through the bar to the back room, where they hold church. Dark holds the door open for me, then shuts us both inside.

Leaning my lower back against the table in the center of the room, Dark posts in front of closed double doors. "Fog came out."

"I know."

"He's dating Lace."

"I know."

"I don't like it."

"The dating Lace?" I guess.

Cracking his knuckles, Dark's nostrils flare. "Yeah. Lace. I wasn't expecting that. But I'm glad he finally told us."

"Me, too."

"I always thought we'd be together the day he came out, and it wouldn't be like this." He gestures between us as if that somehow explains everything.

"We are together." Just because Fog didn't sit us down together doesn't mean he didn't tell us both on the same day in the same place. That's pretty much the same thing to me.

"Not like that, babe." Dark sighs. "You know what I mean. I don't fuckin' like that our son didn't tell us at the same time. *And* I really fuckin' hate that you're standin' over there when I'm here." He points to where I am and then to himself. "It doesn't feel right. It's never felt fuckin' right. I love you. I love you so goddamn much." Slamming his head against the wooden door, it rattles on impact as Dark's eyes squeeze shut like he's in physical pain. "Fuck."

"Dark. Don't do this," I plead, knowing good and well where this will lead if he doesn't stop now.

"How can I not?" His throat bobs as he swallows hard. "You're my wife. Every damn day, all I ever think about is missing you." Pissed at himself, Dark slams his head against the door a second time and curses under his breath, fisting both hands down at his sides.

"Stop. Please." *Stop hurting yourself. Stop putting me through this over and over again.*

"Kali. No. You don't get it."

I grip the edge of the table on either side of me. "But I do. I'm the woman you left. The woman who gets to live next to you while you live your new life with your new family. I get it. Our son came out. I'm proud of him. I know you're proud of him, too. Stop making this more than it is. This isn't about us. This is about him and the job we have to do. We need to focus on that and our kids. That's it. Let it go."

"Kali."

Swallowing down a hot branding iron of pain, I palm my stomach as if talking to him physically hurts. Right now. It does. I don't want to do this. "Dark. Let. It. Go," I beg because I don't want today ruined with memories of us, our baggage, our issues. This is about catching up with our kids, friends, and our son's news.

Refusing to spend another moment locked in this room

with him, I approach the door. Dark doesn't hesitate to step to the side to let me leave. For that, I'm grateful.

Rejoining our family is a breath of fresh air. It's just what I need.

For the rest of the day, it's us at the bar, eating, drinking, and soaking up the now. We eat homemade pie and shoot pool, even though I lose each time. Axel calls in a few more brothers, and soon the place is swarming with Sacred Sinners. Drunken antics aside, the day bleeds into a fun night, and when I finally pour my tired body into the back of an Uber, I'm smiling the entire ride home. When I fall asleep, that same smile is still in place.

NINE

Dark

RELAXING in my leather office chair, foot propped on my knee, I stare out of my floor-to-ceiling wall of windows from my sixteenth-story office that overlooks the bustling cityscape below. The sky is bright blue today, not a cloud to be seen for miles.

A knock sounds at my door.

"Come in," I call out as I watch a woman the size of an ant scurry across the street with her child in hand.

The *click click click* of heels hit my hardwood floor as they approach my desk. "Sir," a sensual voice purrs, drawing a cunning smile to my lips.

Without breaking my view of the world below, I set both feet on the floor, unfasten my trousers, and pull out my hardening cock. "You know what to do." I motion to my member, and she knows exactly what I require as she drops to her knees and swallows me whole.

It's part of my world… This world… Where Dark is dead and Maxim Drake lives.

In four short days, Kali will meet this man for the very first time. Let's hope she doesn't run before I can catch her. My wife is in for the ride of her fucking life.

When I fist the hair of the woman blowing me, it's Kali's brown hair I see, her eyes that look up at me, and that sensual red mouth I explode into.

Because whether she likes it or not… Whether she believes it or not… Kali's mine.

TEN

In T-minus eighteen hours, it's showtime. Lined up on the dock in a long row of similarly dressed crew members, two of Mr. Cassiano's muscle-bound brutes give us orders for our weekend cruise. Tomorrow morning, we upgrade from his two-stateroom yacht to a small luxury cruise ship with enough staterooms to sleep twenty-six. The two female hires and I are in charge of keeping the new visitors comfortable, with whatever means necessary, as the rest of the crew keep everything else running smoothly. At no surprise to me, we're the only females working this cruise. The rest are trusted male employees of Mr. Cassiano's, including Romeo and his two sous chefs.

"We will all meet back here at six a.m. sharp," the tallest of the men instructs, reading from a clipboard. "You will have the rest of today off to pack a bag and get a good night's rest. Everything you bring aboard will be inspected for safety and confidentiality reasons. Unless you're given permission, cell phones or other electronic devices will not be permitted on board."

In other words, they don't want photos leaked or us calling for help when shit pops off. Which it will. It's an illegal auction of literal humans. Not that I'm supposed to know that. Neither are the two other female employees. It's just a party for the rich with their companions—that's the schtick they're selling us. Let's see how well these other two take the news once they see it's an auction. I'm prepared for anything—from naked, drugged-up women to a vile sex cult party. You never know what'll happen. With Dark present as millionaire Maxim Drake, at least I know he'll have my back.

After handing each of us over our assignments in packet form, we're dismissed, and I walk straight to my favorite coffee shop at the boardwalk for a tea and warm chocolate croissant. Carrying my fresh matcha and buttery pastry to a small booth in the corner, I'm so engrossed in reading the paperwork that I nearly knock over my drink when Romeo claims the seat across from me with a coffee and a smirk.

"Hola," he greets, sipping from the edge of his to-go cup.

I rasp a choppy, "Hello," clutching my chest.

Romeo good-naturedly chuckles at my discomfort. "Sorry I startled you."

Shaking my head, I wave him off. "It's okay. I was focused."

"Riveting, hmm?" He nods toward the paperwork.

"It's a lot." I slap the thick stack of papers on the tabletop.

Leaning in, Romeo sets his cup to the side and urges me closer with the crook of his finger. I follow his movements, curious what he has to say. "That packet won't tell you…" Romeo whispers, looking at the instructions between us. "But you need to stay away from the visitors. Keep a low profile. If you think El Jefe's parties were… bad before." His dark eyes bore into mine. "This weekend… extra bad. *Comprende*?"

Pressing my lips together, eyes widening for show, I nod once. "Yes. I understand."

"You need me. You come. I'll keep you safe." Having said what he needed to say, Romeo sits back in his seat and drinks his coffee.

"Thank you," I reply, and I mean it. I believe Romeo when he claims he wants to keep me safe. There's a reason he's been extra nice the past week. Since I returned from my weekend visit with my sons, the chef has cooked for me nonstop, to the point he sent me home with leftovers, which he's never done before. Romeo's treating me like they do when they send pigs off to be slaughtered. You fatten them up. In this case, I sense it's the guilt because he knows what's coming—to be killed or sold. Those are my options. If only he knew the truth. But he will soon enough.

In companionable silence, I read, drink, and nibble on my pastry as Romeo watches me and other patrons mill about the café. When I'm through, we depart together, and he escorts me like a gentleman back to my apartment complex, where I don't invite him inside.

Standing outside the security gate, I wring my hands together, chew the inside of my cheek, and stare up at him shyly. This is what I do. I know I'm playing my part to a T when Romeo steps in, and I step back until I'm pinned against the gate. He's in my space, staring down at my lips as if he can't decide if he wants to fuck them or kiss them. His nostrils flare wide as he inhales and grips the bars on either side of my head.

"Romeo." I faux shiver as he presses in further to show me what I'm doing to his body.

Romeo squeezes his eyes shut and groans as if his name upon my lips pains him.

I trail the tip of my finger down the side of his neck. "Romeo." I speak his name like a prayer, and he stiffens, blowing out a frustrated breath, fanning my face in the fragrant black coffee as if he's battling an internal war. There is no fraternization allowed between employees. That was made clear the day I took this job. I'm sure it's also been made clear to Romeo, given how long he has worked for Mr. Cassiano.

Growling under his breath, Romeo leans down and drags the tip of his nose up the side of my cheek. I shiver when his lips pause at my temple, and he whispers, "Be safe and remember, come to me." Then he's gone, striding away as if it's the hardest thing he's ever had to do. I watch him go to be sure he won't see the code I punch into the gate as I return to my apartment, wearing the biggest smile. Not because I'm into Romeo, because I'm not, but because he's into me, and that's a win. This isn't like the stalkers. This is mission security. This is having an unlikely ally. Even with Dark on board, I can't guarantee my own safety, but with Romeo on my side, I've got a little extra backup, just in case.

Will I share this newfound knowledge with Dark? Nope. This is between me and Romeo.

My personal cell phone rings as soon as I set my purse on the kitchen counter.

Rolling my eyes, I collect it from the nightstand in my bedroom and answer it without looking at the screen. "Stop checking the cameras, Dark. It's creepy."

"Who was the man at the gate, Kali?" he seethes.

Dragging a hand down my face, I sit on the edge of my

mattress and sigh. "Of course, you also put cameras outside my apartment, you fuckin' stalker."

"Answer the question, Kali."

"That's the head chef, Romeo. Shouldn't you already know that?"

"He almost fuckin' kissed you."

"But he didn't."

"His lips touched you."

"I'm hanging up now, Dark."

"Kali. Is there something going on there?"

Sheesh. This man needs to get a grip.

I bark a sharp, awkward laugh. "I'm working a job with my nosy, overprotective ex-husband, who is basically stalking me. I can't even change my clothes outside of my bathroom because of the cameras he installed inside my apartment because he's a *control freak.*"

"You can, too, change your clothes," he defends, as if that's the most preposterous thing he's ever heard me say.

"No. I can't," I argue.

"I've already seen all of you naked, babe. Or did you forget you're my wife?"

Ugh!

"Shut up, Dark. I *was* your wife. I'm not anymore. I don't know how many more times I have to remind you of that. And I'm not letting you see any of me naked if I can help it."

"Kali."

"I'm hanging up. I'll see you tomorrow. Remember?"

"Please be safe."

"I am."

"No more seducing men. That's not part of the assignment," he scolds.

"Goodbye, Dark." Rolling my eyes for what feels like the billionth time, I hang up before he can say another word, and then I fling myself on the mattress dramatically. Can he see me? Sure, he can. The fucker probably watches me sleep like the crazy stalker he's become.

I'll be glad once this assignment is over and I can return to my normal life—watching movies with Lily, eating popcorn, running my shop, and taking care of my plants—back to the simple, relaxing life, back to sleeping in my own bed and seeing Sunshine.

Speaking of Sunshine.

Swiping through my texts, I ignore the litany of nonsense from Dark and click Sunshine's thread.

Him: Play it smart this weekend. You've got this. Miss you, Sweets.

Me: Miss you, too. Are you coming to visit next weekend?

Him: I wouldn't miss it.

Me: What are you doing right now?

Him: Rubbing the last amethyst you gave me.

Pressing my lips together, I stave off a smile as my stomach swirls with weird, girlish emotions at the fact he's using the crystal I gave him. Not that I expected anything different. As I've said before, Sunshine has a cup full of them in his van. But it's the little things like him reminding me he's using them, that they matter to him, it feels… nice. Well, maybe nice isn't the correct word. You know what I mean.

Me: Is that all you're doing?

Him: I'm driving to my next job.

Me: Busy week?

Him: Always is.

I wanna ask what makes it busy, but I know I can't. He can't tell me what he's doing any more than I can share details of what I'm doing—not yet, anyhow. Maybe when I get home, we can talk, and I'll share the sordid details. Until then, I have to keep my head in the game. This is literal life or death.

Me: I'm gonna shower and pack my bag for the yacht. Drive safe. See you next weekend.

Him: Will do. Love you.

Me: Love you, too.

The shower is quick, and the bag I pack is simple—all the essentials I need for my stay, including my two ribbed vibrators, a few changes of clothes, and feminine essentials. It fits perfectly in my backpack that I set by the front door. In another bag, I pack my personal phone, which I power down, and the rest of the items I want to take home with me. I leave the rest of my work clothes, food, and everything else in my apartment because it would be suspicious if I didn't. The shampoo stays in the shower—a razor on the sink. The little touches will make it seem normal when Mr. Cassiano sends his goons to clear out my apartment to make me disappear.

After I finish another dinner of leftovers on my small couch and watch a rerun of *Friends*, I dress in all black, shoulder my personal bag, and duck out of the apartment under the guise of darkness, taking the back ways through town, down darkened alleys and quiet neighborhoods, per Dark's previous instructions. I lock my bag inside a locker downtown, next to the bus station, to be picked up later, and take a different route home to avoid being followed.

Back inside the safety of my apartment, I walk around the small place to appreciate my last night here. Sure, it isn't much, but it served its purpose. It felt like home after a wild day at the office—or, in this case, the yacht.

In the bathroom, I change out of my dark clothes and into a Cami and boy-short panties before I return to the bedroom for a good night's rest. Ha. Like that'll happen. The night before any big assignment, my brain refuses to shut down. It overanalyzes everything, trying to figure out how tomorrow will play out in a million different ways. To fix this, I sit cross-legged on the center of the mattress, close my eyes, and meditate.

Through my nose, I breathe, pulling air into my diaphragm, down into my belly, where I hold it for a count, then release it between my lips in a steady stream of air. My brain clears as I focus on nothing but my breath. The tension I was carrying fades to nothingness. Peace flows through me as I switch from breathwork to a mix of humming and quietly reciting mantras I practiced with my mother when we sat in the grass, the sun on our faces, and became one with Mother Earth, where anything is possible.

I run through the paces until I'm left with a clear head and a peaceful heart. Only then do I click off my bedside lamp, shimmy under the covers, and sleep like the dead.

ELEVEN

Dropping my backpack on my bunk in our shared stateroom after a lengthy check-in process and walk-through of the luxury yacht, I unpack what I need to start the day. We travel into open waters in less than an hour. The men and women are currently being loaded onboard as the three of us dress for a day on the water. Catering to a group of rich, egotistical, handsy assholes happens to be my specialty. Sure, I haven't worked on an assignment quite like this. Not with as many moving parts and people involved. But I've played the dutiful, flirty waitress at underground poker nights. I've sat at tables with men far scarier than you can imagine and held my own. The biggest difference is Dark—his presence. We've done smaller jobs together where I was his partner in crime. His side piece. The arm candy. Pretending I don't know a man who is pretending to be a totally different man is nerve-racking, but I've got this.

In the small bathroom connected to the stateroom, I undress from my standard work outfit into something more flattering—a burnt-orange, long-sleeved, body-con dress that fits like a glove. It hugs my curves in all the right places, and the neckline is just low enough my cleavage will make a man or two drool. Provocative yet classy is the style, and I think I pull it off when I gather my clothes and reenter the bedroom to have both of my much younger companions gape at me as if they haven't seen a woman in a dress before.

"Hannah." Clutching a shirt to her chest, the blonde's big blue eyes nearly pop out of her skull.

I twirl around barefoot. "Does it work?"

"I don't think Mr. Cassiano will be pleased," the bustier, darker-haired blonde sneers.

Not caring what they think, I shrug and set my dirty clothes on the end of my bunk to be dealt with later. From inside my bag, I extract my matching lace-up gladiator sandals. A pair of pumps would pair best with a dress this sexy, but doting on men on a moving vessel could be a disaster in heels. These are the next best thing. Sitting on the small couch beside a built-in vanity, I slide them up, tighten the straps, and flex my black polished toes as the other two ladies finish dressing in their far more modest attire—a white blouse with black flowy slacks and the other a blue pants suit.

A hefty knock vibrates the door. "It's show time, ladies," a goon announces. "Dining room in twenty."

The two women smile at each other, eagerness lighting their faces. "This is so exciting," one says as her friend nods enthusiastically.

Exciting, my ass.

These poor women are about to be traumatized. If I had the luxury of befriending actual people on assignments, I would feel bad about what's coming. But the only thing I care about is keeping them alive. Their mental state will come afterward when we get off this ship, still breathing. The goal is not to become fish food.

As they chatter incessantly about whoever rich and famous might be aboard, I carry my toiletry bag to the bathroom to fix my chignon and apply makeup—real makeup this time. Much to Mr. Cassiano's preferred au natural look, I flip him the middle finger when I rock a sultry, smokey eye and a glossy, nude lip. He will either be pissed I didn't fall in line or be pleased I took the initiative to be an atlas moth in a group of dagger moths. Standing out is the objective. The less attention paid to these two, the better the outcome for them. Not that the blonde, I believe her name's Jasmin, cares much. She's been sucking Mr. Cassiano's cock for weeks. If she doesn't blow him in front of all the men present tonight, I'll be surprised.

Once I'm ready, I lead the charge out of our shared room, through the halls I've yet to familiarize myself with, and up a flight of stairs to the main level, where Romeo and his sous chefs are mingling with the group of sharply dressed businessmen as they drink at the bar in the main dining room.

Wearing the biggest, kindest smile, Romeo waves us over, and I fall in line, ready to serve however needed.

"Jasmin." He hands the blonde a tray of tapas to serve, and she blends into the crowd like a pro.

"Dee." He hands the less-than-friendly blonde a tray of champagne, and she joins her friend in the throng.

Once they're gone, Romeo ushers me behind the bar and grips my elbow. "What on earth are you wearing?" Brow furrowed in the center, his gaze rakes up and down my form.

Suddenly self-conscious, I run a hand down my side. "A dress," I whisper, harsher than I intend.

"You should go change."

"I'm fine." I shrug off his grip and turn to find a familiar face leaning both elbows on the bar, staring daggers at Romeo, his lips pressed together, forming a fine line.

Busying myself with work, I set a white napkin with a foiled C stamped in the center in front of none other than Maxim Drake. "What can I get you, sir?" I bat my pretty eyelashes and smile like a bubbly server.

Romeo curses behind me but doesn't cause a scene.

Dark's penetrating eyes rove over my body like he wants to eat me for dessert, and I shiver at the attention. He licks his lips as he leans in to order his drink. "Mojito," he purrs.

Inwardly, I groan, knowing damn well Dark doesn't want a mojito. Outwardly, I smile even wider until my cheeks hurt and get to work without questioning why he always has to be a pain in my ass. In a cocktail shaker, I muddle leaves of mint to extract their oils, and because I hate making this drink and he knows I hate it, I put extra strength into pulverizing the mint, which I wouldn't do for anyone besides him.

As I make his cocktail, my ex turns, leans an elbow on the bar, and converses with another millionaire I don't recognize. They seem to know each other well when they break into a fit of deep, masculine laughter, and the older man with salt-and-pepper hair clasps Dark on the shoulder.

I dump rum, lime juice, and simple syrup into the cocktail shaker with a scoop of ice, and then I shake the hell out of it. When I'm through, I pour the chilled concoction into a pretty glass and set it on Maxim's napkin. Still engrossed in his conversation, he lifts his drink in appreciation, then lifts it to his lips to sip. I incline my head in acknowledgment and fall into a peaceful rhythm of bartending.

Romeo returns sometime later and sets a small dish on

the bar back with a slice of cake on top, and my mouth waters, looking at its infinite layers. "For you." He juts his chin at the treat.

"Thanks." I wink over my shoulder, then crack the top off a bottle of foreign beer and pour it into a glass for a handsome man with full lips and the kindest honey-colored eyes. Too bad he's a piece of trash like the rest of these men.

I set his glass on another white C-stamped napkin, and he catches my wrist to keep me from leaving. "What's your name?"

Chewing the inside of my cheek, I do my best to muster shyness at being noticed and giggle awkwardly when I reply, "Hannah."

He strokes the inside of my wrist with his thumb. "I hope this isn't too forward, Hannah, but you look stunning in that dress."

Shielding my eyes, I press my lips together to stave off a smile. Again, it's for show. My dress is doing what I intended it to do. If my options are to be sold or killed—I'd much prefer sold, and the more eyes I have on me, the more vying for my attention, the better. I'm willing to bet Dark wouldn't agree. But if I've learned anything in my forty years on this earth, when men have their shields lowered because they feel safe, they are the first to lead every decision with their dick. This yacht and the false sense of security it offers is the perfect place for men to let their proverbial hair down—if you catch my drift.

This weekend is all about indulging their baser desires.

Noticing one of his guests flirting with the barkeep, Mr. Cassiano joins us. "Hannah," he greets.

"Sir." I bow my head out of respect, and the man preens.

Turning toward his host to chat, the man with the kind

eyes continues to stroke the inside of my wrist, refusing to set me free. Out of my periphery, I watch Dark slide onto a different stool, three spots down. He lifts his glass as if he wants a refill, but I can't leave.

"How much?" the man asks my boss, who snorts a mocking laugh and drinks his whiskey.

I pretend I know nothing of which they speak as the honey-eyed man frowns, and his grip around my wrist turns from sweet to iron. I try not to wince.

"I'm serious," the man growls lowly at his host.

Not at all affected by the outward display of small dick energy, Darmond Cassiano firmly pats his guest on the shoulder. "Let Hannah go, Elden. She's here to work. We can discuss numbers *after* the auction."

A grumbling Elden complies, but not before he raises my hand to his lips and kisses the top of each finger. Dying a little on the inside, I pretend to be charmed by it. "I'll see you later tonight, sweetheart." He grins and disappears back into the small group of similarly dressed men.

"Have a great night, handsome," I reply to his retreating form as I slide down the bar to help Dark with his empty.

Setting his glass in the sink to be cleaned, my ex taps his fingers along the shiny bar top. His eyes narrow on me. "Another mojito?" I ask, too brightly.

Dark's head shakes. "No. Just a beer."

"Imported or domestic?"

"Surprise me." The slightest smirk kicks up at the corner of his mouth like it's a dare. *Pft.* As if I don't know what he likes. I might be an ass about the mojito because I had a snooty customer come into the winery, and that's all they drank for hours. Eventually, the pungent aroma of fresh mint made me queasy, even though mint is supposed to have the opposite effect. That's why I don't like them. They also take forever to make.

Kneeling by the beer fridge, I riffle through our bottled options, careful not to break any glass, and find the perfect stout. I open the bottle and pour it into a tall glass. Drinking beer from a bottle at events like this is frowned upon. These men are far too uppity to put their lips to a bottle. Whatever. It is what it is.

The early afternoon plays much the same. I fill the men's drinks as the other two cater to their other needs. When lunch is served, the men fill their seats at the round tables in the dining hall, and I sit at the bar to enjoy my slice of cake.

Romeo appears and sets a plate of whatever he's serving the men beside me. "Sorry about earlier." He pats my forearm and disappears back into the kitchen. The fancy salad with shaved steak is delicious as I eat alone and sip from a glass of ice water.

When I'm through, I carry my plates back into the kitchen, where Romeo's… As I round the corner into the brightly lit room, my feet stutter to a surprised stop, and I nearly drop the dishes. What the hell?

Trying not to make a sound, not even to breathe, I slowly back away, not wanting to disturb them. Because that'd be awkward. A moan erupts from a sous chef, the very male sous chef, as Romeo fucks him over the kitchen counter, where all our meals were just prepared. Alright. I didn't see that one coming. Maybe he's bi. Maybe he doesn't care about the no fraternization. Maybe he had a scratch that needed to be itched. Not that I care either way. This is… weird.

Scurrying back to the bar, I set my used dishes in the sink and busy myself with washing cups and prepping garnishes. I can't believe that just happened. Romeo and the sous chef. The sous chef and Romeo. A young sous chef at that. Wow.

As I rack the wet cups to air dry, Mr. Cassiano approaches the bar and clears his throat to grab my attention.

"How can I help you, sir?" I hang my towel over the now-empty sink, clasp my hands in front of me, and turn on a friendly smile.

"We have an auction we will be running shortly. I want you to refresh the men's drinks throughout our business dealings."

"No problem, sir."

"Please *do not* make a scene. I would hate for there to be any misunderstandings. Do you understand?" he emphasizes, as if this has gone poorly before.

In other words, if you don't like us peddling flesh and you cause any problems, I will kill you myself.

Gotcha. Read that loud and clear. Behave. Be subservient. Smile. Now that I can do.

"Yes, sir. I am happy to help in any way I can." I lie straight through my teeth, knowing what's coming at the end of this sicko's little venture. That's what keeps the smile pasted on my face. That's what excites me.

Pleased with my reply, Darmond double knocks on the bar top. "Thank you, Hannah."

"Anytime, sir."

TWELVE

Round tables are pushed to the outer walls, just below the windows, and the dining hall's center transforms into an auction house. A middle-aged man with slicked-back hair that I've never seen before stands behind a podium at the front of the group. Every businessman sits with a numbered paddle, including Dark. Balancing a tray of drinks on one hand, I pause in front of each of the guests for them to claim their beverage of choice. Jasmin and Dee are nowhere to be found as Darmond's goons post in front of the exits, as if they're afraid the poor women they're about to sell will try to run. Something in my gut tells me that's happened before.

"Thanks, Hannah," Dark whispers as he grabs his beer and shoots me the sexiest, panty-melting smile that would have any other woman's ovaries ovulating double-time. Returning his sentiment with a far more subdued grin of my own, I move on to Elden, my admirer. The man is practically salivating as I lower the tray to eye level for him to nab his beer. He reaches around and caresses my ass. Feigning shyness, I giggle as if he's being a naughty, naughty man, and I like it, when I'd rather stab him in the neck with a fork.

"Thank you. Don't be a stranger, now." Elden removes his expensive import from the tray, and I wink at him before I move on to the last two men, who are less interested in me and far more intrigued with the young, naked redhead being escorted to the center of the room.

With a meaty hand wrapped around her upper arm, Darmond's buff goon orders the woman to firmly "Stay" before leaving the poor thing as eye candy for the entire group of perverts. The redhead couldn't be any older than nineteen, possibly not even legal. Not that they care. As I return to the bar, I remain neutral to her presence, and the auctioneer gives an overview of what they're buying, as if she's not a living, breathing human but a product.

Disgusting.

"Nina, age eighteen. She has been training with us for three years now. Nina is proficient in oral sex, cleaning, and cooking. She rarely acts out of turn and is most happy when her pussy is serviced."

Swallowing down the bile rising in my throat, I remain poker-faced as I clench both fists down at my sides. These assholes are getting hard over this girl while all I want to do is throw a blanket over her shoulders, feed her cake, and tell her everything is gonna be okay. After I'm done here, she will be. But the shit she's already gone through… I can't imagine. Each time I meet a new one of my sisters, it never ceases to amaze me the horrors they've endured, and this poor girl has handled more than most. This is why I came today. She is why I'm here, as is the blonde with the small breasts who comes after her and the Indigenous woman with silky black hair that kisses the top of her ass. As each woman is purchased, she's immediately claimed by her owner and placed either in his lap or on a satin pillow next to his feet as he awaits the next female to be auctioned.

Dark raises his paddle now and again but always bows out a few bids shy of winning. Mr. Cassiano watches the men from the comfort of his chair, sipping a glass of red, like he doesn't have a care in the world.

It isn't until a porcelain-skinned woman with the blondest hair and biggest, bright blue eyes I've ever seen enters that I sense a shift in the room. The wolves are ready to pounce as Darmond's goon deposits her in the center of the auction space, and the auctioneer orders her to make a slow turn. Arms down at her sides, the woman does as she's told, and her large, perfectly shaped breasts bounce with the movement. She's stunning. What's worse, the men know it, as those without a new companion sit forward in their seats, ready to drop fat stacks of cash to take her home.

Even Dark mimics their excitement when he removes his suit jacket and casually drapes it over the back of his chair. Perching on the edge of his seat, he rubs his palms together like he's ready to win this one. The gray-haired guy beside him, the one he was chatting with at the bar earlier, who's currently playing nipple touchy with his new purchase, leans over to pat Dark on the shoulder in encouragement.

"This is Ellie, age nineteen." The auctioneer winks, and I know for certain, along with the rest of the assholes, that she's underage. "Ellie has been training with us for six years."

I squeeze my eyes shut at that knowledge as a pained breath stutters out of me. Holy fuck. That is young.

The man continues, "Ellie speaks three languages, is brilliant at math, excels at oral sex, loves to cook and clean, and is a beautiful dancer. She prefers to spend most of her time indoors but enjoys swimming. She loves double penetration and is happy to be shared."

Alright.

I don't think I can do this anymore.

This is too fucking much.

She doesn't love double… ick, I can't even say the words. They've groomed her and turned her into this man-pleasing vessel when she's a person with likes and dislikes, hopes and dreams, not a fucking product.

Needing a stiff drink to get through the rest of the day, I pour three fingers deep of the strongest, most expensive whiskey I can find in the bottle display and guzzle it down with my back to the auction. My throat burns like battery acid, and I wince as the potent heat pools in my belly.

One more day. Only one more day.

I can do this.

The bids rise for Ellie faster than any of the women before.

"One hundred and fifty thousand. Do I hear two hundred thousand?" the auctioneer calls.

As I turn to face the music again, Ellie stares at her toes, and the men go wild as I wait with bated breath to see who wins.

A nerdy businessman violently stands from his chair. It flies back a few feet before it topples over. "Five hundred thousand dollars." He thrusts his paddle in the air as the bulge in his pants shows exactly what he wants from this young woman.

Dark stands, too, and sneers at his rival. "One million," he growls, flashing his number—*323*.

A ripple of unease works its way through me at how

convincing my ex is to win. If I didn't know any better, I'd say he was just as into this as the rest of the group.

The auctioneer smiles like a villain in a horror movie. "Do I hear two?"

The number grows and grows. One man drops out, then the next. By six million, we're down to three players—Dark, a younger businessman with a crooked nose, and a guy with chunky glasses and a beer belly.

"Do I hear seven million?" the auctioneer calls.

Emitting a loud, unhappy sigh, crooked nose man retakes his chair, where he slumps as if he lost the magical key to the sex traffickers' World of Wonder.

A cruel smirk claims Dark's lips as he nods in appreciation at the guy for bowing out.

It becomes a battle of wills. By ten million, I grow more uncomfortable and tap my foot on the rubber mat behind the bar as my ex continues to bid with a wicked cockiness only Dark can muster. This wasn't what we discussed. Is he going off-script because of her beauty, or is this part of the script I wasn't informed of? Where does this leave me if he wins?

By fifteen million, glasses man concedes. "Too rich for my blood," he announces, and I watch in horror as my ex saunters to the center of the room, kisses the girl on the cheek, secures her by the elbow, and steers her from the makeshift auction space directly over to Darmond, who's still seated.

"For you," Dark offers, pushing the blonde forward.

My boss's eyes widen to the size of the moon as the girl smoothly drops to her knees at his feet. "Max," he gasps in genuine surprise, shaking his head at Dark's generosity.

"Consider this a gift," my ex explains. Not *her,* a gift. *This.* An object. A thing.

Darmond scoots forward in his chair and cups the beautiful blonde's cheek as she kneels on the floor between his parted legs. Ellie leans into his touch as if it's second nature. All the men watching fall madly in love with her submission while I'm trying not to throw up at how genuine she looks in accepting his affection. Ellie's lashes flutter before her eyes drop to a soft close as the smallest of smiles warms her porcelain face. She acts as if she's home, and that's when I realize most of these girls believe these men are their saviors. That they are on their way up in the world. This is what they trained for—to be bought.

Not questioning Maxim Drake's motives because, apparently, Darmond knows something I don't, my boss covets his new prize by ordering his goons to escort Jasmin and Dee back into the room. Opening the fly of his pants, my boss pulls out his hardening cock and snaps his fingers at my coworkers. "Clothes. Off."

Not missing a beat, the auctioneer carries on with the next commodity as Dark reclaims his seat, fifteen million dollars lighter. I can't believe he did that. Remind me to ask him why when I get a chance. There must be a reason other than blondes being Darmond's preference.

Having been our boss's sexual outlet for the past month, Jasmin removes her clothes without protest as Dee looks to me for help. Knowing I'm of no use to her right now, I shrug and busy myself with another round of drinks for the men.

"You. Eat her pussy, and you, suck my dick," I overhear as I lift my tray laden with drinks. With a sensual sway of my hips, I round the bar to reenter the auction ring.

"Your wine, sir." I carefully pluck the glass from the

group. One wrong move, and I'll have a floor covered in broken glass and alcohol. Good thing this isn't the first time I've served drinks to a group of men.

The businessman accepts his merlot with a pleasant smile as he pets the hair of the Indigenous woman curled naked at his feet.

"May I get anything for your companion?" I offer, not wanting to cross any lines.

"No, thank you. That will be all for now." The man cuffs his hand around the back of his purchase's neck as I float about the room, delivering each man's preferred beverage and asking if his companion would like anything. All of them decline the offer.

Passing over the foursome as they're in the throes of debauchery, I quickly deliver Dark's drink and move on to Elden, who stands as I approach, takes my tray, deposits it on a table a few steps behind his chair, and retakes his seat, where he pats his lap. "Sit," he orders.

Wringing my fingers in front of me, I chew the inside of my cheek, worried this is the worst idea yet. Elden hasn't purchased a woman. Elden was waiting for me to return. With sexual tension thick in the air and the tight state of his pants, that's all I need to know about his intentions. But I have to sit, even though I don't want to, because nobody here will come to my rescue. Not even Dark, or he risks blowing his cover.

Smiling as if I'm pleased as punch to be picked, I lower myself onto Elden's knee, and the man moans, actually moans, as my ass settles on the firmness of his muscled thigh. Like a creeper, he presses his nose to the side of my throat, and I giggle cutely as if I love him sniffing me.

Kill me now.

"You're gorgeous." He licks a stripe up my neck to the shell of my ear, where he nibbles there, and I gasp, not from pleasure but discomfort. Though, I do my best to act like I'm interested when I rest my hand on his other thigh and quell the urge to sock him in the dick.

"Fuck," he groans, removing my hand from his leg to place it over his erection. "I'm gonna have fun with you tonight."

Like hell, he will.

I say nothing as he manually uses me to rub his cock over his pants.

Another woman is sold as I fall into myself, disassociating from what I'm doing in favor of peace. I play Hannah, the submissive employee, and make sexy little noises when he gropes my breast and continues to stroke his member with my hand. It's average as wetness blooms through the fabric, coating my palm with precum.

"I can't wait to fuck you," Elden moans at my throat, on the cusp of making a sticky mess in his slacks.

Someone roughly clears their throat, and I glance over my shoulder, expecting to see a pissed-off Dark about to cause a scene. Instead, I find my boss standing beside our chair, and he looks like he's about to commit murder.

"Hannah, you may go." Darmond dismisses me with the swish of his hand, and I do just that. Head hanging low as if I've been scolded, I retrieve my discarded tray and scurry to my place behind the bar, secretly grateful for the interference.

I wash my hands in the sink and scrub them until they almost bleed as Darmond puts Elden in his place. "Did you buy her?" he seethes.

Elden says nothing.

"I didn't think so. Hannah is under my employ. She does what *I* tell her to do. She acts in my best interest. Did we broker a deal?"

Still, Elden remains quiet.

"No. Of course, we haven't." My boss snaps his fingers. "Fred, take thirty million from Elden's safe," he orders the auctioneer.

Without speaking, the man behind the podium scribbles something on a ledger and puts on a spectacle when he slams a stamp down on whatever he's written. "Done." The auctioneer's voice booms through the room.

Elden's mouth gapes from his seat. "That's bullshit—thirty million." His voice cracks.

"You know the rules. You brought the money. You signed the agreement. You were invited to my private event and treated my employee like she was yours. Hannah is not yours. But..." Darmond pauses for effect and taps a ringed finger to the center of his lips. "I suppose, for your donation to our special charity, I cannot, in good faith, leave you without something in return." Once more, my boss snaps his fingers. "Dee. Come," he commands like she's a dog.

Still naked, Dee rises from her spot on the floor next to Mr. Cassiano's chair and approaches the men. My boss points to Elden's lap. "He's now your master."

Surprised by the news, Dee squawks in outrage, and I flinch prematurely, knowing exactly what's going to happen. Quick as a snake strike, Darmond backhands her across the face, and the entire room reverberates with the violence. My teeth clench as I watch her absorb the hit, head flinging to the side, as water wells in her eyes and her skin turns crimson, already starting to swell.

"Keep your bitch in order," he snaps at Elden. "By any

means necessary." Then the powerful man turns to stalk off and immediately connects eyes with me behind the bar. His nostrils flare in annoyance as his gaze swings from me to the doorway, where we both look to find a red-faced Romeo.

Darmond says nothing as he glares at his chef. The tension ratchets up a handful of notches before my boss's dark gaze shifts back to me, narrows, and a cunning smile pulls at the corners of his lips.

My breath falters as fear seizes in my chest. This cannot be good.

Blinking once to break his intense stare, my boss sweeps his gaze across the room of men. By some miracle handed down by Mother Earth, he stops on Dark. "You." He lifts his chin at my ex-husband. "What was mine is now yours. You can thank Elden for buying the gift for you." He turns to face the auctioneer. "Make it happen."

More writing and stamping follows. Then the deal is done. I'm sold.

Dark doesn't seem the least bit fazed as he inclines his head in appreciation at Elden and my boss. "She's no Ellie, but thanks for the gift."

Pleased with the ass-kissing compliment, my boss looks at the blonde sitting pretty at the base of his chair beside Jasmin. "Enjoy her," he comments to Dark as he retakes his seat. With a sweep of his hand, Darmond gestures to the auctioneer to get on with it, and they do, picking right back up where they left off.

Romeo approaches me behind the bar as I rinse more empties in the sink, not sure if I'm supposed to keep working or sit by Dark. "Hannah, I'm sorry."

"It's okay." I smile tightly and set a wine glass on the rack to dry.

"Mr. Drake is a cruel man," Romeo announces, more to himself than me.

Dark would be the man to build his empire on the façade of brutality. His dark hair, gray eyes, muscular build, and tattoos make him the perfect fit for that narrative. It's smart. Damn smart. The weaker men will fear him, and the stronger men want to be him. Dark is nothing if not brilliant. Trust me, I didn't fall in love with him all those years ago just because of his looks. It's what's inside that made me fall hard. It's a shame all those years were a waste. Well, not a waste. We got two amazing sons out of it, and now we have Lily, and I can't imagine a life without her in it.

I hum in response to Romeo's comment.

He moves in closer. "Hannah."

"It's fine." I jerk away when he brushes the back of my arm.

"It's not. You should know what you're walking into."

Frowning, I glance at him over my shoulder. "Will it change anything?"

"No."

"Then I don't want to know." Because it won't matter anyhow. The man they know is not the man I know.

"Hannah." The chef touches my shoulder. This time, I don't pull away.

"Let it go, Romeo. It's done."

A string of Spanish expletives trails the chef back into the kitchen as he leaves me to deal with my fate.

I'm now the property of Maxim Drake and shit's about to get realer than real.

Dark is my owner.

I'm never gonna live this down.

THIRTEEN

All the women are now claimed by their masters, and the men are visibly giddy with their shiny new toys. They should be, considering the money they spent to obtain them illegally. Erotic tension swirls like a thick fog around our group as I sit on Dark's lap, where he's ordered me to remain. We're no longer in the dining room but on the covered side of the pool deck, next to the outside bar. After applying liberal amounts of sunscreen, most of the women are currently skinny dipping in the saltwater pool as their owners watch in various states of undress from their loungers, where their oversized umbrellas provide little protection from the bright, mid-afternoon sun. The breeze is perfect on the calm, open water, as we float in the middle of nowhere, not a bird to be seen or another boat for miles.

My back settles against Dark's front. A smile draws to my lips as the brine of the salty air tickles my nose, and my head rests on his bare, muscular shoulder. He unbuttoned and shrugged off his shirt when we claimed this spot. It was a perfect choice, with just enough shade to keep from burning, yet close enough to hear everyone's conversations. Dark drapes each of my legs over his, and my dress draws up, exposing the white lace of my panties underneath. I gasp, wanting to tug the hem down, but I remain unfazed, knowing this is what is expected of me. To follow his lead. He explained as much when we sat in my living room the day he briefed me on the mission.

A tattooed arm wraps around my middle as Dark sets his other elbow on the armrest and draws lazy designs across the side of my breast. His warm breath tickles my ear when he whispers, "You're fuckin' perfect in my lap, babe."

I swallow hard.

How am I supposed to respond when nobody is actively listening? Do I giggle? Do I play shy? Do I play hard to get? There's no way to act natural when none of this is natural. Cameras are all over the boat, so we can't break character. Somehow, this feels a lot like Mr. and Mrs. Smith, without the us being together part.

Trailing his tongue across the side of my neck, I stiffen in Dark's lap as my heart leaps into my throat. A hard cock I'd recognize in any lineup thickens against my spine.

"I've got you," Dark rumbles hotly before his mouth finds purchase on my neck and sucks hard, so hard my toes curl in my gladiator sandals as I grip his thigh and bite back a traitorous moan. I can't believe this is happening.

Squeezing my eyes shut, Dark's rich scent, mixed with bergamot and lavender, makes me want to scream at him for not preparing me for this closeness, for this level of acting, as he envelops me in the familiar cocoon of his body heat, I was not prepared for.

Because I didn't know this would happen. I didn't think.

I'm stupid. So damn stupid.

I should have known.

I should have expected it, given Darmond's reputation and the nature of our job.

Because I have no other choice, I play along as my cheating ex-husband sucks welts at the pulse point in my neck. His hand guides between my parted thighs, and I try to clench them shut, but he doesn't let me. Widening his posture widens mine and exposes even more of me to the onlookers, if they're even paying attention.

Dark drags a finger along the seam of my panties. "I've got you," he repeats, as if I need a reminder that he has me. Sure, he has me in his lap. He's branding my throat in possessive hickeys, and I hate him for it. I hate him for everything.

When his finger nudges the scrap of fabric shielding my pussy, my eyes slam shut in equal parts mortification and need. I haven't gotten off in forever, and I haven't been touched like this in… nine-plus years. He knows me. He knows which buttons to push. He knows what my body needs and how it needs it. Sex was never an issue in our marriage. Nothing really was beyond the normal marital problems everyone has.

Cuffing his hand around my throat, Dark locks me in place as his finger glides beneath the lace of my thong.

Goosebumps break across my flesh. I gasp at his boldness.

The pad of Dark's finger slides effortlessly through the wetness and into my core, where he stuffs not one but two fingers. A deep rumble battles in his chest, vibrating through my back as the pressure around my throat tightens.

I die a little.

Because this is too much.

I… I don't know if I can do this here, with him.

"I've got you," he vows again, as if that changes anything. It doesn't. We aren't together. This is my body, and I know I agreed to follow his lead, but this wasn't what I had in mind.

He was the man I loved.

The man I planned to spend the rest of my days with.

But he's not anymore.

After his deception, I vowed I'd never let him touch me again, not like this. Yet here we are. I'm at his mercy.

Dark's fingers curl inside me and press against the spot that leaves me gasping for breath as a ripple of intense pleasure forces me to shiver against my will.

"I-I…" Words stutter from my lips, but I die a painful death when I can't think of a response that won't break character. Instead, I sink my nails into Dark's forearm and scream inside my head for him to stop, to cover me up, to let me go. But as I apply pressure to his arm, his fingers start to thrust in slow, torturous pleasure as the palm of his hand presses down on my clit.

The bastard kisses the side of my face. "I'm sorry," he utters as the steel rod against my back bucks, and he fucks me in front of everyone. Plunging his digits in and out of my core, Dark puts on a show, giving Darmond and his group of sickos exactly what they want, what they expect.

Eyes rake my form from the deck. I sense them like ghostly fingertips brushing my skin against my will.

"Let go," Dark encourages.

I can't.

I'm mad at him and myself for this. For everything.

The top of my dress is ripped down, exposing both of my breasts to the crowd. The cool, salty breeze caresses my nipples, setting them to stone. My center clenches around Dark's fingers.

"That's it, babe. That's it." He squeezes my throat until my head spins and the world blots out. Heat coils in my pussy, coaxing, coaxing, coaxing that special spot to come.

"That's it," Dark rasps again as I go limp in his arms. Only then does he release my throat enough to let the blood flow freely, and I'm a goner.

Slamming his fingers home, my back arches off Dark's chest as a scream rips from my throat. Wetness gushes from my pussy. Quaking in his embrace, Dark doesn't relent. He plays my body like a fiddle and fucks me harder, beating that special place like a maestro.

Someone gasps nearby.

The sound barely registers over the pounding in my ears.

"Another," the bastard declares.

And I obey.

A Pavlovian response, my body bows to his command as a tidal wave of ecstasy tears another scream from my broken soul, and I come and come and come with his fingers inside me and his palm grinding against my clit.

"Fuck." Sinking his teeth into my shoulder, Dark grunts as his body thrusts like it has no control over itself. Air bursts from his nose as he trembles, sending violent ripples through us both. The fingers inside my pussy still as the thighs beneath me stiffen and wetness soaks through the back of my dress.

I just…

I….

I exhale an emotional breath.

The hand around my throat drops to cup my breast as Dark nuzzles his nose to the mark on my shoulder and the brands around my neck. "Fuck." He kisses me everywhere, sweet pecks of satiation, as the body beneath me goes lax as if he's been tense all day, and coming in his pants was just what the doctor ordered.

I can't believe… never mind… it doesn't matter.

Head resting on his shoulder, I stare up at the wooden ceiling as my ex plays with my nipple and draws his fingers out of my core to rub my clit.

I gasp.

He laughs like a menace.

"Wanna go again, babe?"

I shake my head. No. Definitely no. This was enough—too much. Later, when we leave the yacht and return to our lives, we'll have words, heated words. Until then, I'll play the part. I'll smile and be the submissive pet. I'll be Dark's. Tomorrow, when we're riding home, I can break. Because this, him touching me, reminding me of what we once had and what he stole away, will wreck me. I sense it brewing below my breastbone. It aches. The wound, mostly scabbed over and healed, has been ripped open. Now, it's gaping. Bleeding. I hate him for it, now more than ever before. How could I have ever been so stupid?

FOURTEEN

Cutting steak into bite-sized pieces, Dark stabs a succulent bit with his fork and raises it to my lips. Smiling like I'm smitten with him and his gentlemanly ways, I slide my lips sensually across the tines and draw the steak into my mouth. I chew thoughtfully, and he stabs another juicy, medium-rare piece for himself. Playing the dutiful pet, I turn in his lap to pat his lips with a white cotton napkin as he chews.

"Thank you." He smirks and leans in to press a simple kiss upon my mouth. My eyelids flutter at the connection, the sizzle, the flutter in my belly. Not done, Dark draws his tongue across the seam. I gasp, core clenching as he hums in deep, hungry satisfaction. "You're fuckin' perfect," he mutters.

The compliment soaks into me like a sponge, into places it doesn't belong, and for a moment, I believe it's genuine. For a moment, it's just us, our lips, and our dinner. The others drinking, feeding, and fucking their pets are background noise to the heat of his body seeping into mine and the wisp of his breath fanning over my lips as mine part to taste where his tongue touched. Shyness mixed with a thousand other unwelcomed feelings burn my cheeks as Dark turns me in the chair with little effort and drapes my legs over his lap to give him better access to my mouth.

"I need this." He whispers a breath before sealing the soft warmth of his lips over mine. The kiss is sweet. It's perfection. It's Hell. But I'm far too drunk on expensive wine to care.

Dark's touch lingers for what feels like forever. His breath fans my face, scented with beer. Turning into him, I rest my palm on his thick pec, and he groans as if it's painful to be touched.

Neither of us move.

Neither of us press for more.

It's us and the kiss.

Simple.

My heart thuds harder and harder as a murder of crows takes flight in my belly. Dark's hand presses my shoulder, and I gasp at the simple touch, breaking the spell. Noises flood back in of moans and groans, happy chatter, and knives scraping plates.

Dark hums in deep contentment as he draws away, lids heavy, wearing the sexiest, lopsided, punch-drunk grin I've ever beheld.

And I'm done for.

That smile.

Those impossibly beautiful eyes.

My resolve crumbles to ash at my feet, and I let him touch, kiss, and feed me. We've played this game of cat and mouse for hours, and this mouse is exhausted.

He wins.

I give up.

After the pool, I collected my things from my stateroom to bring to his and changed into another dress, a white virginal-looking baby doll style with poofy sleeves. He swapped out his messy suit for a green Henley and dark denim jeans. We've been inseparable since. I sat at his feet during a poker game and curled in his lap over drinks with the men. Now we're back in the dining room, no longer an employee but his plaything.

Romeo served filet mignon for dinner with a fancy, buttery, garlicky potato masterpiece and a side of asparagus. One plate for us both. Unlike the others, Dark is happy to share. Because, unlike the others, he also gives a genuine shit about me. Which is odd when you think about it, given our unusual relationship.

When he returned from his run with Lily and Abby in tow, nothing stopped him from moving on with his life, moving somewhere else, starting a new family, and never looking back. Men do that. Make new lives with new women. But he didn't. He moved two houses down and tried to be a father to the boys and a friend to me. Even if he's annoying sometimes, that doesn't stop it from being true. All my stereotypical male household needs are met between him and Sunshine—roof repairs, car maintenance, lawn mowing, gutter cleaning, and even raking leaves in the fall. I don't have to ask. It just gets done. Just as I don't have to ask for my wine to be replenished as the vicious Maxim Drake snaps his fingers, and just like that, my cup is refilled by Romeo, who refuses to look at me out of anger or something else entirely. I guess I'll never know.

When the lithe, blond sous chef I saw Romeo screwing pauses at our side of the table, Dark asks me, "Are you full, babe?"

I nod, melting into him, letting him hold my weight.

"We're done." Dark swishes his hand for the sous chef to collect our plate.

Across from us, the gray-haired man Dark was chatting with at the bar fucks his dark-haired pet over the table. Her bare tits bounce with each thrust, and I stiffen at the closeness of their debauchery. I've never been one to participate in public sex. Not that I care if anyone else does. It's Darmond's kink, and something tells me it's one of the many reasons these men purchase women from him the way they do.

My ex grips my chin and forces me to look at him. "Eyes on me."

I want to ask why, though it's not like it matters. I've seen sex parties before over the past month, maybe not this close, but on the periphery of Mr. Cassiano's weekend gatherings.

"Has anyone ever told you, you have a perfect body?" Dark asks, and I blush. I know it's because it's unexpected, but my eyes widen in surprise anyhow, and he chuckles.

"No?" he prompts, waggling his dark brows. "Well, whoever you've been with before was a dumb fool for ever letting you slip away."

He's not wrong. He was a dumb fool.

"I didn't slip," I remind him.

"No?"

I shake my head. "Nope. He cheated."

"Idiot." Dark huffs, smirking like a sex symbol.

"My thoughts exactly."

"His loss."

"I know." On that, we agree.

"My gain." He winks in a flirty, I-should-want-to-kill-him-but-don't way. Ever the fool, I press my lips together to keep from smiling. Because, of course, Dark would say that. His gain. Ha. He's the asshole who got us into this mess in the first place.

"I suppose so," I deadpan, and he throws his head back and barks a deep, rumbly laugh. His entire body vibrates beneath mine, tugging the smallest grin to my lips. He's such an idiot—an unbelievably hot one—but still an idiot. He'll pay for this. Oh, will he pay. Becoming his plaything will come at a price.

To prove as much, I grip the outline of his cock over the front of his pants. It's far bolder than I should be given our history, but sometimes a girl has gotta do what a girl's gotta do. My touch morphs Dark's laughter into a long, throaty groan.

"Babe," he grits through his teeth.

"Hmm?" I act innocent when we know I'm anything but.

His nostrils flare, and somehow, even that's sexy. It must be the wine talking. "What the hell are you doin'?" Dark's eyebrow hikes in question.

"I don't know. What *am* I doin'?" I play coy as he thickens beneath my ministrations.

"Not here."

"Why not?"

"You're drunk."

Pft. Like that's ever stopped him before.

"Not that drunk," I remark, though I am pretty drunk.

"Christ." The curse is a prayer upon his lips.

"This is what you want, isn't it?" I massage his cockhead through the denim. He wants compliance. He wants sex party sex. I'm merely doing what is expected of me.

Eyes squeezing shut as if he's in agony, Dark's head shakes. "No."

"No?" I scrape my nail around his crown. Teasing. Taunting. Driving him mad.

"I said, fuckin' no," Dark snarls, ripping my hand off his thickness. Shoving his chair back from the table with me still seated on him, he abruptly turns me around, forcing me to straddle him. My outer thighs cut into the chair arm, and my dress draws up as Dark's hands cup on either side of my face, and his eyes bore into mine.

"Wh—" I begin but am abruptly cut off.

"Look at me."

"I am."

"Keep your eyes on me," he stresses, holding my head firmly so I can't move it even if I want to without causing a scene.

I understand why when the screaming starts.

"No!" a female wails, and my eyes round in horror as a different woman screams—Dee. I'd know that voice anywhere.

Pressing my lips together, I chew the inside of my cheek as the familiar sound of fists pounding flesh erupts.

"Babe." Dark jostles me to ensure I'm paying attention to him when all I can do is zero in on the sounds. I can't help it.

Tears well in my eyes.

"Don't fuckin' look."

I nod just enough for him to understand that I promise not to as the first woman's shrill scream makes my ears ring.

"No. No. No! Don't! Please!" Dee begs.

There's a harsh slap, fists, and then the snapping of something. An eerie chill tingles my spine as I keep my eyes on Dark, only Dark. His thumbs draw circles across my cheeks, and that's when I realize I'm openly crying, and he's wiping away the evidence.

"That'll teach you, bitch," Elden roars, and I stiffen at the cold, cruelness in his voice. He's a monster.

"Eyes, babe. I've got you," Dark reminds me, showing little emotion—as if he's cold as ice, as cold as Elden. According to Romeo, he is. Is this what Dark does, too, when I'm not around? Do I want to know? Do I believe he could do such a thing? No. But… his face is unreadable.

Fuck, women are being hurt, and I can't help them.

He can't help them.

We're sitting ducks as someone chokes in pain before a wheeze pours from their lips.

"I—"

"Shhh." Dark cuts me off with a firm shake of his head. "No. Talking."

Okay.

I won't.

Dark's brow wrinkles in the middle as he watches both me and something over my shoulder.

"I'm sorry," a different woman says to who I assume is Elden.

"When I said stick my dick in your ass, I fuckin' meant it, bitch!" the monster roars.

The woman wheezes again.

Someone snaps their fingers.

"Give him your gun," Darmond announces.

My back goes ramrod straight, and I grip the bottom part of Dark's shirt, twisting it in my fist.

What's the gun for?

What's the gun for?! My eyes beg Dark to tell me, to make it stop, to make them stop. They can't… can they? They wouldn't… right?

"Shhh. You're mine. I've got you, babe. You're mine," my ex whispers harshly.

Another rush of tears trickles down my cheeks, and he brushes them away with the pad of his thumbs.

"Please. No. I said I was sorry!" Dee screeches. "Please!"

"I'd rather fuck you when you're dead," Elden states with no inflection in his tone, just like a serial killer, and I jump as the gun unloads once, twice.

Fuck.

Dee's dead.

He… he killed her.

"You are safe," Dark reminds. "You. Are. Safe." He jostles my shoulders to get his point across.

But I'm not safe. Not really. That man is a fucking monster. If I took this job on my own without Dark, that could have been me.

I overhear Elden speak to Darmond and his men.

"Clean up the mess," the boss orders.

"Bring the body to my room," Elden requests.

"You're sure?" Darmond asks.

Don't say yes. Don't say yes.

"Yes. I paid fifteen million for this bitch. The least she can do is take my cum."

My lips waver as even Dark's eyes round in disbelief.

"Very well." Darmond snaps his fingers, and I hear his goons move into action.

"Cover her head," Elden orders.

"Yes, sir," one of Darmond's men responds.

Chin dropping to my chest, I blow out an emotional breath as the scent of pennies suffuses the air. The men clean up Elden's mess before carting the corpse to Elden's room.

"Sorry about that, everyone." Darmond laughs

awkwardly. "It doesn't usually come to that." He clears his throat. "Bring in the dessert, Chef."

As if Dee wasn't killed and another woman hurt, dinner and dessert resume. The sous chefs fill drinks and deliver sweets by the plateful.

Dark hooks a finger under my chin to force me to look at him. "Babe."

"Yes?" I croak, voice thick with emotion.

He wipes away what's left of my tears. "I want to shower and fuck you," he announces loud enough the people at the table can hear. Then, in a lower tone, he leans in and whispers, "We need some time alone."

Yes.

Time alone.

Away from these men.

Time to plan.

Time to get my head on straight.

Time to sober up.

Offering a shallow nod, I agree with this plan, and Dark snaps his fingers like Darmond.

A sous chef rushes to our side. "Sir?" the younger male asks, standing at attention.

Rubbing his fingers up and down my sides to calm me, Dark looks up at the chef. "We'd like a tray of all the desserts you've prepared tonight. Deliver it to my room."

"Every dessert, sir?"

Dark purses his lips for half a beat as if he's irritated by the male questioning him. "Yes. Is that a problem?" he growls.

"No. No," the young chef recovers quickly. "It's just we've prepared ten different kinds."

"Then deliver the ten," Dark states, as if that shouldn't be an issue.

"Yes. Sir. No problem." The sous chef scurries away, and Dark turns his attention back to me. Gripping my sides, he helps me to my feet, then smooths out the sides of my dress when I stand. He offers me the crook of his elbow and flicks his gaze there. "Ready?"

I slide my arm through his. "Yes, sir."

"You're leaving so soon?" Darmond asks as he approaches us with his new prize in tow.

"Yes. That was…" Dark hums in his throat, trying to find the right word.

"Unexpected?" Darmond supplies.

My ex nods as if that word fits just right when that isn't the word I'd use. "Yes, unexpected. I don't want that to ruin the mood, so we'll have dessert in my room."

"Dessert, eh?" Darmond smiles as if dessert is code for something else entirely.

"Yes," Dark confirms and pats my arm tucked through his. "A dessert to pair with my other dessert."

"I like the way you think, Max." Darmond pulls his pet in front of him, her back to his front, and cups her large breasts.

Not sparing the woman a single glance, Dark barks a laugh. "Let's just hope she can suck cock just as good when it's covered in cake."

"Yes. Let's hope," Darmond replies with a chuckle and bids us a goodnight.

Knowing where to go, Dark leads the way back to our stateroom. Once inside, he locks our door and presses a finger to his lips, indicating I shouldn't speak.

Not sure where he's going with this, I nod in understanding as he groans and stretches both arms over his head. "Man, that was an eventful day. We should shower before I get your lips around my dick." Raising both brows, Dark gestures for me to reply.

Oh. Right.

"Sounds great, sir." I pull the response out of my ass, wondering why we're still acting our parts in the confines of the bedroom.

"Great. Let's get you washed up." Not missing a beat, Dark tugs his shirt over his head, hot-man style, by tugging the back over his head, and my mouth almost comes unhinged at the sight of all those muscles and tattoos on full display as he unbuttons his jeans and tugs them, along with his boxer briefs, down to his feet in one swoop. Then he unlaces and pulls his boots off. I watch it all. Because this man has gotten far hotter with age. The six-pack he had when we got married is still very much there. Only the groves are somehow deeper, yet he has a thicker layer of just enough cushion over them. I don't know how that works, but damn, it looks like any woman's wettest of wet dreams, and now I have to shower with this body.

Not paying a lick of attention to my less-than-objective perusal, Dark folds his clothes neatly into a pile and sets his boots in the corner. Then he looks up to see me still dressed, and that's when I get the biggest eyeful of... everything. Sweet Mother Earth, what is she feeding this man? Did he sell his soul to the Devil to look like that?

Redness blots Dark's cheeks when he notices me noticing him. His cock twitches. Not that it has to do much. He's always been a shower. You know those men who wear sweats, and you can see their entire thing outlined? That's him. Only it's about twice in length and extra girthy once he's hard. I don't want to say this because it's totally wrong, but he and his father are hung the same. Not that I'd tell either of them that. Unless they brought it up themselves. Like father, like son—in most departments. Eek.

"Babe," Dark croaks, covering his growing member with both hands as he sways uncomfortably.

Only then do I blink out of my hot-man trance and peek up at his face.

"If you keep lookin' at me like that, you're gonna end up with my dick inside you in the next thirty seconds. Get naked and meet me in the shower." Grumbling to himself, my ex walks with a purpose into the bathroom. His bare feet slap the tiled floor as he turns on the shower. I do as I'm told—slip out of my dress, bra, and panties, as my insides go haywire, and my pussy… purrs.

This is a bad idea.

It's a very, very, very bad idea.

Gathering my clothes, I set them and my boob rocks on the small couch to deal with later and turn to face the open bathroom door. Clenching both hands down at my sides, my feet fuse to the floor. If I go in there, I'm going to be naked, fully naked, with my ex. He hasn't seen me nude since… you know when. I'm older now. My body isn't what it once was. I'm not like the others. Sure, with my clothes on, they cover up the imperfections, and normally I wouldn't even give a shit, but this is… I don't even have words for what this is. It's heavy. There. That's what it is. Heavy.

"Babe. Get your ass in here," Dark calls from under the shower spray.

I stall because maybe he'll get out once he starts to prune, and then I won't have to stand in a small shower stall, sharing water with my ex-husband, his intoxicating male scent, those muscles, that ass, and just… all of it, trapped in there behind the glass door.

No amount of alcohol or talking myself up will make this any less embarrassing and less… heavy.

"Now. Babe. The water is hot."

If that water is hot, that means Dark wants to shower with me, and he's willing to bathe in the waters of hell to do it. Dark likes warm water, the tepid kind—not water that leaves your skin ready to peel off. That's a woman thing.

His loud curses jolt me into action.

I don't want to fight, and I did promise to follow his lead.

In the bathroom, I approach the stall like a turtle. *Shuffle. Shuffle. Shuffle.* I stare at my feet, not at the clear glass.

"Shut the door, would ya? Don't want to let all the steam out," he calls.

Following his orders, I do just that. Once we're locked in together, he pushes open the door, and I look up. Under the spray of water and the overhead canned light, there's the man I fell madly in love with and that smile reaches into me and fists my heart as his cock bobs hard and inviting in front of him.

When I look closer, because there's a lot of yummy man to ogle, there's a tattoo by his… member.

A pair of red lips.

Those weren't there the last time we had intimate relations, which can only mean…

Oh.

Fuck.

I take a step back as reality crashes down on my shoulders.

He's Abby's.

He's cheating on his woman with me.

I've now become the other woman.

I'm the home-wrecker.

My back hits the door as I retreat, and Dark's out of the shower in a flash. "Babe." His arms wrap around me, his face in the crook of my neck as I begin to sob. It's unexpected and ugly.

I'm the other woman.

I'm hurting Abby.

What have I done?

What. Have. I. Done?

"In the shower. Now." Dark drags me against my will into the steam and under the rush of hot water.

"I'm the other woman," I whisper in horror, hands trembling at my sides.

"Fuck. Babe. No. No. Fuck. No." Securing my face in his hands, Dark forces me to look at him. No matter how hard I fight him and try to wrench away, I have nowhere to go. My back is pressed against the far side of the shower, too far from the door, and his impossibly big body crowds me. "You can talk in here. The room is bugged. Just be quiet. Only whisper. The water will drown out the noise."

"I…" A pained hiccup tears from my throat.

"Aw. Sweetheart. You've done so fuckin' good today. I'm so fuckin' proud of you."

"You…" I glance down at Abby's lips and back to his face.

"Ah. Shit." Dark rubs the tattoo with two fingers and squeezes his eyes shut. "It's not what you think. I can explain."

"You…" Trying to regain my composure, my bottom lip wobbles. "Don't have to explain. She's your… You know."

"Wait. What?" He pauses a beat before those gray eyes

finally round in realization. "No. Noooo. Shit. These aren't Abby's lips. They're yours." He pats the tattoo right there, next to his very erect dick.

"They're what?" I whisper-screech.

"Yours."

I frown so hard my face hurts. "No, they're not." That's not possible.

"Yes. They are." The asshole chuckles as if I'm ridiculous, and he thinks it's cute. Any second now, he'll pinch my cheek, and I'll bite his finger off like a rabid dog. "Do you remember you used to put cards in my bag before I left for a run? You kissed the cards. I had Pix make a copy and tattoo it on me. It's the same size and everything."

"You tattooed my lips by your..." I gesture to his anatomy. This isn't happening. This isn't real. Those cannot be my lips. He's a complete fucking idiot if they are. Though, I do remember putting cards in his bag before a run. It was our little thing. I did it for Sunshine, too. A bag of healthy snacks, a crystal, and a card or note. Nothing sappy. Just quick and sweet to remind him who he was missing when he was gone because I missed him like crazy when he left.

"Yeah. Why wouldn't I?" He looks at me as if this is perfectly acceptable and I'm the crazy, irrational one.

"We aren't together," I remind him for the billionth time.

"You're my wife." Dark sighs as if he's tired of having to repeat himself. "You will always be my wife."

That's not how it works. "Dark," I start, but he slashes his hand through the air.

"Enough. Not now. Not here. You can kick my ass tomorrow. Okay? I wanted to bring you in here so we can talk. So, I can see how you're doing, given how today went."

So that's what we're talking about. Fine.

"You kissed me and put your fingers in places you don't belong. How do you think I feel?" Used. Oddly satisfied. Violated… and a smidge icky. That about sums it up.

Leaning into my space, as if he could get any closer, he slaps a hand against the shower wall above my head. "You know I had to. Right?"

"I do. But you didn't warn me."

"I know, and I'm sorry."

"Are you really?"

"Honestly?"

I roll my eyes. Since when do I not want honesty? "Yes. Obviously."

"Well. Then. No. I'm not sorry that I got to make my wife come again after almost a fuckin' decade. No. I'm not sorry I got to kiss you. Just as I'm not gonna be sorry when you suck chocolate cake off my dick or when I fuck you tonight."

That's definitely not happening.

"We aren't having sex, Dark." I press my palm to the center of his wet chest and stand my ground.

"We have to, or Darmond will think something's up. He's gonna listen in. He might even jack off to your moans. The guy might like blondes, but don't think for a second he doesn't have a sweet spot for you. I've known the man for years. He isn't nice to his female employees."

"And you sent me here anyway, knowing that?" I hiss and suppress the urge to knee him in the balls. Because who does that?

"I had a hunch."

"No, you didn't," I argue.

"Yeah. I did. Do you think I'd take you away from Lily for a month and risk your safety on a whim?"

When he puts it that way…

"Well. No," I relent, even though I don't want to. Dark won't put me in danger on a whim. Even if he hated me, I'm the mother of his sons, and that means something to him.

He cocks his head to the side in that cute, dog-like curiosity. "Do you think anyone else could have worked this job as well as you?"

"I guess not." I shrug. Someone could probably do a better job, but I don't know that person, so maybe not.

Staring at my breasts as the water washes down the front of me, Dark pushes my wet hair over my shoulders, and I shiver despite the moist heat. "You can be pissed at me tomorrow after you finish the job. Tonight, I need you to be Hannah. Suck my dick. Let me fuck you. Yeah?" As if he can't help himself, he reaches out a tentative finger to touch my nipple. I slap his pervy hand away, and his stupid erect cock twitches as if he likes the attention.

I cross both arms over my breasts so he stops staring. "I don't want to fuck you."

Truth.

I don't want to.

It complicates things.

This is already complicated enough.

"Sweetheart." Once again, the jerk looks at me like I'm cute, and it does nothing but make my hackles rise.

"What?" I glare, knowing damn well he's gonna say something stupid.

Dark brackets his hands on the wall on either side of my head and looks down at me from his imposing height. "Do I need to say it? It's gonna make me sound like an asshole."

Refusing to be intimidated by anyone, especially him, I tip my head back and meet his cocky gaze with a fire stoking my own. "You're already an asshole. So, you might as well say whatever you wanna say."

"Who knows your body better than I do?" His brows waggle suggestively.

Oh. Fuck him. That's a low blow. I know it. He knows it. That's not fair.

"Shut up," I growl.

A single brow arches, and the tiniest smirk hooks at the corner of Dark's lip. "Admit it," he goads like the dick he is.

A high-pitched, irritated noise wrenches out of my throat. "Fine." I shove him in the chest, but the bastard doesn't move an inch. "That might be half-true," I lie. It's more than half-true. It's true. You don't spend two decades with a man and him not know your body inside and out.

Dark draws a single finger down my cheek and neck. Stopping at my collarbone, he traces across the delicate line and down the front of my chest to the valley between my breasts. "Then let me do what I do best. It doesn't have to mean anything to you. It's just sex. It's just a cock." Said member flexes and brushes my stomach.

"You mean touch the world's biggest asshole's cock?" I snort at my terrible jibe, then sober because this is serious. "You know I'm gonna need therapy after this, right? I was celibate for two years after what you did. I've only just started having regular sex in the last year or so. This is gonna—"

"Be amazing," he finishes with a cavalier smile that shouldn't be as panty-melting as it is.

"No."

"Yes." To further prove a point, Dark presses his heavy, muscled body to mine and traps his hardened length against my belly. His eyes bore into me. "I love you. Let your husband take care of his wife."

"I hate you," I mutter.

My ex shakes his head as if he doesn't believe me. "Consent, Kali. Give it to me. Tell me. Dark, I want you to fuck me. Dark, I want your cock in my mouth."

"No." I turn my head away, unable to look at him. I don't want to. I don't want to say anything. I want him to go away.

He drags his nose up my cheek and pauses at my ear, where he whispers, "Say. It."

"No." I'd rather swallow the semen of a thousand whale dicks than say it.

Nipping my lobe, Dark draws back, grips my throat, and forces me to look at him. "Tell me, dammit." He applies pressure. Just a little. A squeeze. An assertion of dominance.

Swallowing under his hold, I blink up at him in defiance. No. I won't tell him. I won't agree to this. Even if my pussy clenches in need. Even if I want him in my mouth again. I hate him for making me even want it. I hate him for everything. Why do I still find him attractive? Even that's annoying and pisses me off.

Not backing down, my ex puts his face in mine. "I will fuck you tonight. You will come on my cock. Do you hear me, you stubborn, fuckin' woman? Do you fuckin' hear me?"

"Try it," I dare. Try. It.

It's one thing to get away with fingering me in public, where I can't break character. It's quite another when we're in the bedroom together. Where I have the upper hand. Angry with this entire day, I bite his bottom lip. Snapping it between my teeth, I draw blood, and Dark moans so loud the sound reverberates through the bathroom as he grinds his cock against my wet stomach.

The metallic tang lingers on my tongue as I reach up and grip his throat, too. I don't know who moves first, me or him, but the tension snaps like a rubber band, and suddenly we're kissing, tongues dueling for supremacy, as we touch everywhere. His hands grip my ass and lift me until I wrap my legs around his waist. His cock nestles against my pussy lips as we fumble out of the shower and drip water across the floor, our mouths fused in explosive hunger.

In the bedroom, Dark drops my back onto the bed with a bounce, and he's there with me. Reaching between us, he pulls back just enough to sheath himself in my heat, and I'm a goner. Neck elongating, my eyes slam shut, and I sob into our kiss as he drives home. It's glorious. It's hell. It's the best worst decision of my life, but right now, I don't care. I wrap my legs around him, dig my heels into his muscular ass, shut off the logical parts of my brain, and let him have his way with me, consequences and guilt be damned.

"Fuck," Dark growls into our kiss. "Fuck." He wrenches his lips away and stares down at me. A tear leaks out of the corner of his eye. "Fuck." He swallows thickly and licks his bottom lip, where I drew blood.

Not wanting him to ruin the moment by talking or acknowledging what we're doing, I brush his tear away as if it doesn't exist and smile softly. "Come here." I lock my fingers around the nape of his tattooed neck and draw him closer. Dark doesn't fight me when his chest connects with mine, and his heart pounds through my breasts.

I nudge his nose with my own. "Kiss me, you fool."

Expelling a deep, needy groan, my ex does just that. Uniting his lips with mine, I'm transported to our bed, where we made love. Where he didn't hurt me. His big palm cups my ass as he tilts my hips up to hit that sweet spot and grinds his pelvis against my clit. Moaning into his mouth, we both struggle to draw breath as my ex fucks me into the mattress with glorious thrust after thrust. The bed squeaks. Skin slaps skin, and he fills me like nobody else can.

And I love it.

Every moment is just what I need.

What I long for.

When he draws back to suck another mark onto my neck, I hold him there, wanting him to brand me forever, to fuck me forever, to make me come.

"Max," I gasp when he cups my breast and draws a nipple into his mouth. As I glance down at him, he smiles like the wicked man he is and sucks.

My toes curl at the sight, at the shimmer in his gray eyes, at my… husband—the man I used to love with my whole heart. In this moment, he's here with me, drawing pleasure from me because he can, because it's his life's purpose.

"I'm gonna eat your pussy all night, babe. But you gotta come for me first." Dark hooks my legs over his shoulders and drives to the hilt, hitting that spot.

Gripping the bed cover in my fists, my back arches as air stutters out of my chest.

"That's it," he encourages. "Come on my cock."

"I… I…"

"Now," he demands, slamming his hips home. Bending to his will, I shatter into millions of pieces as I scream through my climax. But he doesn't stop. Of course, he doesn't. Dark yanks himself out of my core, and then he's there, licking my pussy and sucking my clit, moaning like it's the best meal he's had in years.

Two fingers curve inside me as he kisses my clit like they're long-lost lovers, and they are because she responds just like he expects, but for me, it's too much, too fast, too sensitive.

"No. Too much," I whimper, heels digging into the bed as I try to scoot away.

Chuckling like a madman, Dark removes his digits to hold me in place and attack my clit.

"No. No." I rip at the covers, trying to get away as everything coils too tight, too much, too, too fucking much. "Please. Stop," I screech and hold my breath as Dark sucks and sucks and sucks on her. "No!" I gasp.

And the bastard. The horrible, horrible man doesn't relent. Not when I writhe on the bed. Not when I pluck violently at my nipples. He sucks and toys with her. He kisses her, and she loves it.

"Please!" I claw at his hands to let go. Desperate for relief.

And it comes.

Oh. It fucking comes.

When Dark lashes my clit and kisses her deeply, he hums in his throat as if he knows this is it. This is the end of me.

And he would be right.

Eyes rolling to the back of my skull, I convulse as a train wreck of the purest pleasure rips through every inch of my soul. Fluid squirts from my center, and Dark moans, lapping it up as I try to stay conscious through my hoarse scream.

The world goes black.

"Babe." Dark pats my cheek.

Shivering, I blink up at him, dazed and unfocused.

The sweetest, cockiest grin quirks at the corner of his swollen lips. "You passed out."

"I did not."

Looking down the length of his muscular form, I zero in on his cock. It's flagged a bit, not fully, but he's not as hard as he once was, and there's no residue of cum, only the sheen of precum on the head of his member.

He didn't even finish, which means…

"I passed out," I amend.

"Yes." He chuckles. "You came really fuckin' hard."

Blinking a dozen times, I wet my lips and heave a wrung-out sigh. "Gee. I wonder why."

"It was stunning. You're stunning." Sitting on the bed beside me, Dark lightly traces his fingers up and down my form. Goosebumps pebble in his wake. When he reaches the apex of my thighs, I squeeze them together to keep him from going any further.

A noise of disapproval percolates in his throat, and he nudges them apart. "Now. Now," he teases, drawing a single digit through my soaked slit to my core, where he swirls around my entrance. "I'm gonna fill you with my cum tonight. But… right now, I'll settle for a kiss and another shower." Leaning over, Dark caresses my lips with his own before dropping the sweetest peck there, and I melt like a fool, because this is… not what I expected. He delivers a second swipe before he rights himself and offers me his hand, palm up, patient and waiting. "Let's go. Do you think you can stand?"

With Dark's help, I sit up and scoot to the edge of the mattress, where he pulls me to my feet, and my legs wobble like a newborn colt. Chuckling to himself, my ex curls an arm around my shoulder as we slowly make our way to the shower, which is still running. Whoopsie.

No words are exchanged this time as we bathe with the complimentary shower supplies. Dark washes himself with a washcloth as I scrub my face and hair. When I move to switch places so he can bathe in hot water, Dark steals my washcloth out of my hand and pumps the neutral-scented body wash on the rag. "Let me wash you." He suds up the cloth and doesn't wait for me to reply when he drags the soapy fabric across my throat and down through the valley of breasts to the intricate tattoo low on my belly, where our birds stand on the skull. He washes my raven with the utmost fascination, then his.

"I miss you," he whispers to himself. "I miss you every day."

My heart clenches at the admission, but I don't respond because there's nothing to say. We have tonight. We don't deserve it, and it's wrong, but we have it. It's here. Things will be different tomorrow, and I'm okay with that. I can move on, knowing we had a moment. And for that special moment, things are good.

Dark cleanses me with care. When he reaches my pussy, he doesn't cross any lines for once and gives her the attention she needs, despite his hard-on.

When we're through, we dry together in the small bathroom, sharing shy looks and small smiles before we return to the bedroom, clean and refreshed. When I sprawl out on the bed, we don't speak as Dark retrieves the chocolate cake from a fancy cart that was somehow delivered when we were otherwise occupied. Naked, I prop myself up on my elbows and watch as he coats his erection in the sugary goodness. With one hand to keep his cock from swinging and making a mess, he uses the other to carry the chocolate cake to the bedside table, where he sets it before he kneels on the bed by my head.

Dark points his frosting-and-cake-coated dick at me and urges me over with the crook of his finger. My mouth waters, and I lick my lips as I scoot closer, my stomach giddy with anticipation. Carefully, as I lay back and tilt my head to the side, he positions himself and presses the tip of his cock to my mouth.

Eyes briefly sliding closed in nervous pleasure, I part my lips and welcome him inside. The tang of precum and chocolate coats my tongue as he slowly fucks into my mouth with shallow thrusts. Dark's thighs quiver as I watch his hooded eyes watch where his cock disappears. His lips part in such wonder, and raspy gasps erupt as the heat of my mouth draws him deeper.

Dark brushes my cheek with such reverence my nose burns with the urge to cry. "Beautiful." He bites his wrecked bottom lip, and I swirl my tongue around his thick glans, gathering all the precum from the tip.

"That's it," he groans, sliding his shaft deeper. "Fuck."

Wanting this to be the best blow job he's had in years, I suck him, lick him, and let him fuck my mouth however he pleases, and it turns me on. My pussy aches, and my clit sparks to life as he uses me, my mouth, my body. I grow hotter and hotter until I can't take it anymore and slip a hand between my legs for relief as my heels dig into the mattress.

Dark bats my touch away. "No. That's for me."

I growl in frustration around his erection.

Tapping my cheek, he gestures to his face. "Up here."

Obeying, I make eye contact.

Pulling his cock from my mouth, Dark traces the bow of my lips with the tip. "I will take care of you, babe. Now suck my dick." He slides in until he breaches the back of my throat, and my eyes widen at the loss of air. Cupping my head, he holds me in place. "It looks pretty in your mouth."

Dark brushes two fingers across the apple of my cheek. "You're gorgeous."

For as long as he desires, Dark fucks my mouth. In and out, slow and steady. His body shudders, his nostrils flare, and he moans but never comes. Over and over, he recoats his shaft in chocolate cake and feeds it to me. I savor it. The flavor, the smooth glide, the connection. I don't think, I feel, and when I rub my legs together, needing some friction, needing more, Dark pulls out, goes to the bathroom, washes up, and returns to fuck me.

All night, we kiss, we connect, and we come.

I lose count of how many times he gets me off.

And when he fills me with cum, I want more.

Need more.

Crave it.

Stomach flat on the bed, his body hovering over mine, Dark's body stiffens as he pours another load into me, and I sigh at the pulse of his cock emptying, at his hot breath on my neck, and his scent, our scent, hanging in the air, making me high, or maybe that's the orgasms talking.

His body still inside mine, Dark cuddles me and peppers kisses across my shoulders as he tries to breathe. "Damn," he huffs, pushing my hair away from my neck to kiss me there. "I'm drained."

"Me, too." I yawn and squeeze my pussy around his shaft. It pops out, and we both groan at the loss.

Taking that as a cue to get up, Dark washes in the bathroom and returns with a warm washcloth moments later. "Roll over," he orders.

Doing as I'm told, I transfer onto my back, and he spreads my legs. Kneeling on the mattress, he pays special care to my lady bits, cleaning and washing them as if they're the most precious thing he's ever seen. When I squeeze down, another rush of cum dribbles out of my center, and he flattens his stomach to the bed and surprises the hell out of me when he licks me clean.

"What are you doing?" I gasp, trying to shove his head away, which gets me nowhere.

"Tasting us." To fortify his statement, Dark runs his tongue through my folds and pays special attention to my entrance, where he spears my well-used hole and presses his palm to my lower belly. I clench down again, and he hums as if I just deposited another morsel for him to savor.

With a final lick, he sits up between my legs and leans over me.

Pressing his lips to mine, he whispers, "Open."

My mouth parts, and his tongue, coated in us, slides over mine. It tastes incredible—salty and sweet. Fresh.

"We taste amazing. Don't we?" He flicks his tongue across my lips.

Savoring us, I nod in lazy agreement because we do.

Heaving a long, sad sigh, my ex drops a final kiss on my lips and retreats. He pushes my legs back together and lounges beside me on the bed. I turn to face him, and he brushes the back of his fingers across my bare breasts. "Tomorrow's gonna be a long day, babe." He absentmindedly swirls a finger around my nipple, and I let him. "We gotta rest. You good if I spoon you naked?"

Not wanting to ruin our night together by feeling feelings or overthinking… my happy, mushy, post-orgasm brain doesn't revolt at sleeping next to Dark, us spooning, or even what we did tonight. Going with it, I turn over and press my ass against his soft cock. Dark throws the thick, white duvet over us and curls around me, his knees pressing into the back of my mine as he sucks and bites another mark into my shoulder before he kisses the sting away.

"Goodnight, beautiful," Dark utters as he presses his palm into the center of my stomach.

I rest my hand over his and give it a gentle squeeze. "Goodnight, Max."

FIFTEEN

After almost a month of living this new life, today's my day, the day I've been waiting for all along. Bouncing on the balls of my bare feet, I stare at myself in the bathroom mirror as the shower and sink run to shield our conversation. Standing beside me, Dark frowns. It's not the normal unhappy kind. This goes a step beyond that. This is worried Dark. This is the Dark that comes out when he is about to stick his foot in his mouth and cause huge issues for us both because his ego and protective nature are screaming at him to stop me.

If this is such a problem for him, he should have considered the risks, the genuine risks, when he roped me into this job in the first place.

I collect a razor blade from the marble vanity and lift it to my cheek.

Dark's hand shoots out to stop me. "No." He steps forward, ready to interfere.

"It has to be done," I whisper, eyeing the conflicted man in the mirror. "Unless you want to backhand me yourself, I need to draw blood. I need a cut and a swollen cheek," I remind him because I must put on an Oscar-winning performance to sell this charade.

"I don't like this." Dark's jaw clenches—the muscles on either side of his face flex as the lines in his neck pop with tension.

"You don't have a choice," I also remind, in case he forgot.

"Babe. Please," the interfering asshole begs with soft, puppy dog eyes.

Frustrated with him, I slam the razor onto the bathroom counter and spin to face him, both arms tucked across my chest. I cock my hip as I stare at the problem. Him.

"Hit me," I challenge, turning my cheek to give him plenty of surface to smack. I had to smuggle that razor blade inside my vibrator. Now, he doesn't want me to use it. Then he has to do something. If it's not that, it's a hand. He needs to pick.

Head rearing back as if I slapped him, Dark looks like he wants to throw up at the suggestion. "Fuck no."

"Then shut the hell up and let me do my job," I growl.

"I don't like this."

"I don't care what you like right now. Got it?"

Turning around like a total pain in the ass, Dark presents me with his back. You know the men who wear form-fitting shirts that seem to cling to all their sculpted muscles? That's him. So now I get a view of his incredible backside as I reclaim the stupid razor blade and get this over with. Slicing my cheek about an inch, I hiss as blood bubbles to the surface and trickles down my pale face. To add to my battered victim façade, I slap myself a few times and collect a bit of blood on the tip of my finger. I use it to coat the inside of one nostril to give the illusion I also had a nosebleed.

Not wanting to appear too obvious, I gather more blood and flick a few dots onto my blush-colored dress. You can't see them from far away, but the specks are there, up close like a subtle misfortune. *Whoopsie, I didn't notice I bled on myself when my new owner beat me.*

"You about done?" Dark grumbles, unable to stand still for even a second. I get it. He's revved up. That makes two of us.

"Are you ready to fight?" I rinse the blade under the water and return it to my makeup bag to hide the evidence.

Dark huffs a slew of quiet curses before he finally answers me. "No."

"Too bad." I turn off the sink and shower before he protests further. On the way out the door, I grab his shirt sleeve and drag the pain in the ass into the main cabin where the bugs are planted.

"Please don't make me," I fake sob, standing in front of my ex. "I'm sore." My voice wobbles for effect.

Glaring at me, his cheeks flushed with anger, Dark punches the air. "I'm not giving you a choice, bitch!" he roars, then winces in shame as he paces the room.

If he wants to sell this, he'll have to do a lot better than that. We have a story to sell here.

Not letting him get away, I shove him hard from behind to turn up his adrenaline and get him into fucking character. We don't have time to waste.

Spinning on me, Dark grabs me by the throat and slams my body into the closest wall. A picture on the wall rattles as I scream in horror, trying like hell not to be turned on by this because I love being manhandled by him, especially the growly, super sexy, pissed-off version of him. The one that oozes strength and sex appeal. The one that could crush my larynx with a squeeze. It does something to my insides. Please don't ask me why. I'm fucked up.

"I said, I'm gonna fuck your ass, you whiny bitch." He punches the wall beside my head hard enough to make a dent, and I gasp, not in shock, but on the cusp of pulling my dress up and letting him do what we both want.

"No. Please! I don't want this!" I cry in fake terror.

Pressing his body against mine, a ripple of pleasure travels through Dark into me. "Bend the fuck over, slut," he growls in that low bass that has the air seizing in my lungs.

The dirty part of me wants to do it. Bend over. Submit. To give him my ass. I'm not sore from last night. I could go another round or twenty. When I woke up this morning, wrapped in a warm blanket of Dark, with his morning wood digging into my backside, I was happy, and I hate myself for it. It's not even about him. It's about me. The intimacy. The trust. Being the other woman. Where I may never trust Dark with my heart or emotions like I once did, I will always trust him with my body because he knows every inch. Concurring with my sentiment, my pussy pulses as if she is entirely on board with getting fucked another dozen times today, but that's not why we're here.

Focusing on the mission, I grapple with Dark. Shoving him in the chest as he pushes me back. Smacking him across the face with my open palm. Redness blooms across his cheek, and we're left panting as we fight. When he slams me against the wall for a second time, I nearly come. He's too fucking much, too sexy, too… everything.

Playing into our scene, I pull up my dress, exposing the top of my thigh, to give him something to smack that won't hurt me for real. With my eyes, I beg him to do it.

"Fuck you!" I spit at him. Well, at the floor, but whoever's listening won't know the difference.

Straightening his shoulders and adjusting the erection in his fancy suit pants, Dark nods once, as if he's resolved to put in a little physical effort. I offer my thigh with a little wiggle, and he doesn't disappoint when he snarls, "Don't fuckin' push me, bitch, or I will kill you!" His palm comes down painfully hard on my thigh. I yelp and stagger to the side to stay upright.

My eyes water, as does my nose, and I breathe through the onslaught of genuine agony. Dark's there, holding me up, looking like he's really gonna throw up this time. I know he wants to ask if I'm okay, but we can't break character. I have to go with it. So, I do. I think of all the awful things he did to break my heart. The first day I saw Abby. The day he ruined us. Using that pain aids a genuine cry. Fat tears roll down my cheeks, and Dark can't take my distress when he threads both hands behind his head and paces the room as he continues to spew fake bullshit to sell the narrative.

"The next time I tell you to take my dick, and you act like this, it will be your last. Do you fuckin' understand? I own you." Taking his jacket off the hook on the wall with a vicious growl, Dark pulls our door open and slams it shut as he departs, rattling the room. Expelling a breath, I set my palm over my pounding heart, close my eyes, and will myself to calm down enough to limp into the bathroom and get a good look at myself in the mirror.

I look amazing.

Red cheeks, swollen, tear-stained eyes, a dried cut, little bits of blood here or there. My hair's purposely mussed, but it looks more like a disheveled mess. In my makeup bag, I extract the most important item of the day—my loose-setting powder.

Inside the front of my dress, between my boobs, I hide it there for later. This dress and bra conceal it well. Not wanting to go today without proper protection, I add three important boob rocks to the underside of my breasts—black onyx for intuition, jade for luck, and blue aventurine for courage and security.

It's showtime.

Before I leave our room, I slip on a pair of blush patent leather flats. Two of Darmond's goons keep a lookout in the hall when I exit, likely doing their rounds. They did that on his personal yacht, so I can only assume they do that here.

Smoothing down both sides of my dress, I swipe the tears from my eyes so they witness me doing it. Then, I steel my shoulders and approach the closest one.

"Has everyone already had breakfast?" I sniffle.

Staring down at me from his substantial height, the goon's brutish face shows no emotion when he replies a simple, "No."

I nod thanks and find my way to the kitchen, where Romeo and his sous chefs are busy preparing breakfast.

Looking up from a plate he's sliding eggs onto, Romeo gasps at the sight of me and rushes to my side. The sweet man drags me to a stool and forces me to sit.

"What the hell happened?" He looks around suspiciously, likely waiting for my owner to claim his property.

Combing a hand through my messy hair, I don't say a word, knowing damn well we are being recorded, and I don't want to cause any trouble.

The back of Romeo's finger caresses my cheek, and I

suck in a sharp, pained breath because it hurts. The cut's raised and swollen, skin tender.

Not pleased, Romeo curses and leaves me long enough to scoop ice into a baggy and wrap it in a towel before he presses it gently to my cheek.

Again, I hiss, this time because it's cold.

"Sorry. Sorry," he apologizes. "You take it."

Following his instruction, I hold the pack to my face as he moves fluidly through the space, finishing breakfast. Outside the kitchen windows is a vast blue sea of gentle waves and a cloudless sky. It's gorgeous out there. Too bad my day had to start like this—with pain and a fight. What's even sadder is these rich bastards get to live like this anytime they want. They wake up on luxury yachts with attractive women by their side. They're fed by some of the best chefs. Yet, they always want more money, more power, more influence, and never stop to appreciate the things that ordinary folks would give their left tit for. Money is wasted on the rich.

"Have you fed the employees?" I ask, knowing Romeo always makes breakfast sandwiches with the option of coffee or bottles of Gatorade. There were mornings when he was busy feeding Darmond's guests so I delivered the employee's food instead of him.

"Not yet. We're running behind." He winces and massages the bridge of his nose before washing his hands and returning to the stove to finish the sausage. It's relaxing watching them work. The flow, the efficiency, the talent.

When Romeo finishes the meat, he sets it on the center island for the sous chefs to work their magic while he sets a cup of orange juice on the counter before me. "It's a mimosa," he explains. "Go slow."

I hum in appreciation.

Orange juice and expensive champagne… I won't say no to that.

Sipping bubbly from a standard glass, I smile politely, ice my cheek, and continue to appreciate their unique dance.

Romeo sets out multiple champagne flutes on a tray, but more is needed for all those being served. Wanting to be of use, I leave my stool and put myself to work. I open another bottle of champagne and fill the bottom half of each glass.

"Hannah. Go sit down. I've got it." Romeo tries to shoo me away with a white kitchen towel.

Head shaking, a soft laugh bubbles out of my throat as I ignore his directive. "Why aren't there more flutes?" I ask.

"The… women aren't allowed to drink alcohol," he answers, whisking something in a steel bowl.

"Oh." The, *but I am*? is somehow communicated without being communicated. Now that I think about it, there wasn't a single woman drinking more than water. No wine. Not even a cocktail. Interesting. Perhaps it's an age thing? I don't know, nor does it matter, I suppose.

Next comes the orange juice, but clumsy ole me accidentally spills it all over the tray—the entire container.

"Dammit." I grab whatever I can to sop up the mess. Ever the valiant man, Romeo's there in a flash, helping me wipe down flutes and transfer them to another tray.

"I'm so sorry." I toss a sodden rag into the sink and collect another to wipe the mess from the side of the cupboard where the juice spilled down, creating a little puddle on the floor.

"It was an accident," Romeo reassures.

Walking over to the sink, I set my orange-stained cloth with its equally stained cousin. "I'll get another orange juice. We have another, don't we?"

"Yes. In the walk-in." He flicks his chin at the closed steel door, lifts the old tray, and dumps what's left of the juice into the sink.

Nodding like a frazzled bobblehead doll, I hurry to the walk-in fridge, where an entire shelf of unopened orange juice cartons sit on a wire shelf. With my back to the door, to shield what I'm about to do, I extract the loose powder from the confines of my dress, unscrew the lid, and set it on the shelf. I open the orange juice and scoop two, okay, three scoops of the powder with the small spoon hidden inside the container. Wasting little time, I return the powder to my dress and turn to leave with the contaminated orange juice just as a sous chef joins me in the walk-in. I sniffle as if I've been crying, and I shuffle past him, head down, hugging the carton of OJ against my chest. He doesn't seem to suspect anything, nor does Romeo when I pour the contents into the flutes. Then, they deliver them to the guests awaiting food in the dining room.

Still pretending to hide from Dark, I don't join the rest of the men and women for breakfast. I need to execute another part of the plan in the next twenty minutes, or all hell will break loose if those carrying the big guns are still conscious. We can't have that, can we?

Once the sous chefs return and resume preparing the employee breakfasts, I collect the bag Romeo uses to transport the sandwiches to the men. Then, I take it upon myself to gather the sports drinks from the walk-in. I perform a little magic as I'm in there, you know, more cap unscrewing, powder dumping, and a little shaky, shaky, so the men will be none the wiser. Collecting the dozen colorful drinks, I stuff them into another tote, and when I return to the kitchen, everyone's almost done.

"Can I help?" I set the bag of contaminated drinks on the island.

"No," Romeo replies, wrapping the sausage, egg, and cheese biscuits with foil to keep them warm. "You shouldn't even be here."

Chewing my bottom lip for show, I gesture to the door that leads to the dining room. "Should I leave?"

Romeo's brows pinch together, and his nose wrinkles as if he sucked a sour grape. "No. Of course not."

Eyes cast downward, I slide my fingers across the smooth edge of the island. "Will you get in trouble? I don't want you to get in trouble. Perhaps I should go back to my room… Or…" I tremble. "I could join *him*," I whisper, as if I'm scared of Dark and what he'll do to me if I return to his side.

"No. You'll have breakfast here." Romeo motions to my vacated stool.

"And you won't get in trouble, right?" Wanting to be useful, I collect a stack of napkins by the window and fold them around the foil-wrapped sandwiches before carefully setting them in their bag.

"I'll handle it," Romeo reassures.

"T-thank you."

The kind chef nods as if no thanks are needed, but his lips thin into a grim line, like he knows this isn't going to end well. Little does he know how right he is—only not in the way he's thinking.

A sous chef pours hot coffee into cups and shoves them into a stackable carrier, and I collect the packets of sugar and creamer.

Naked as the day she was born, Jasmin races into the kitchen, panic written across her face. "We need water and the seasick medication!"

Shit.

The mimosas are working too quickly.

Both sous chefs gather armfuls of water bottles from the walk-in and deliver them to the dining room as Romeo collects the emergency stash of medications. Taking advantage of the distraction, I run with it, shoulder the bag of drinks, sandwiches, and the stack of coffees, and race from the kitchen before Romeo can stop me. In the hall, I pretend to reconfigure everything I'm transporting to make it easier. Huddled in a corner, I pull the powder from my dress, contaminate as many coffees as possible, and set out to deliver the food.

Each goon reaches into the bag, and I hold it for him to grab whatever he'd like. Most men claim at least two sandwiches, a coffee, and a sports drink. Then I'm onto the next, smiling like the polite, submissive worker they think I am.

The wind whips my hair as I climb the outdoor stairs to the wheelhouse, where the captain and co-captain run this giant vessel. I knock on the door before going inside, where I'm met with smiles.

"Hannah, how lovely to see you again," the co-captain greets as I pull two coffees from the stack and set them along with sandwiches and sports drinks on what looks to be a small snack station, complete with jerky, nuts, and other healthier options.

"Enjoy, gentlemen." I half bow like an idiot before I escape the chamber and slowly descend the stairs, a giddiness now churning in my gut. My job is done. The main part, anyhow. The poison I've made will run its course, and soon, the ship will be ours. These rich assholes will be dead, and I can go home.

Death by poison is a little bland compared to a major

shoot-out, I get it, but it's efficient and puts far fewer people at risk. Saving this many women and offing this number of men to hurt Remy's operation couldn't be accomplished any other way. If they had stab wounds or bullet holes, when their dive teams come to retrieve the bodies, they'll see there was foul play and not assume they died from a fire on the water and couldn't escape. It's not perfect, but it's what I was taught to do. My mother was a crazy plant lady and shared much of her knowledge with her only daughter. Where my mother learned her nefarious ways, I'll never know.

Still carrying the empty totes and coffee holders, I return to my stateroom. In the bathroom, I set my items on the counter and pull the small bottle of liquid makeup remover from my makeup bag. In the sewing kit I brought, I slide out three needles that look nothing like a sewing needle because they're not, and finally, I peel back the tabs on three tampon sleeves and remove the syringes I stowed inside. Screwing the needles into place, I use them to suck the liquid from my makeup remover. These are my insurance policies if someone doesn't ingest what I contaminated. It has happened before.

To keep from stabbing myself, I cap the needles and set them inside the bag where the sandwiches were before heading back to the kitchen, where all hell is currently breaking loose.

"Hannah!" Romeo gasps. "Are you okay?"

"Yes. Why?" I set the coffee holders on the kitchen island.

"Everyone's sick."

"Everyone?" I grimace.

"*Sí*. I-I don't know what happened." Romeo fills a bucket of water at the kitchen sink, shaking as he looks at me over his shoulder. His eyes are round with worry as sweat beads on his dark brow.

Wanting to comfort him or appear to, I round the island to offer my support. He's so preoccupied with the water and the sous chefs as they race in and out that he doesn't notice my hand slide into the bag hooked over my shoulder or hear my thumb pop a cap off the needle. Sliding up to the man who has been kind to me, far more than I deserve, given my reason for being here, I pull the syringe from my bag and rest my head on his shoulder.

He hums in contentment as if I'm soothing his woes.

I wait for the guilt of what I'm about to do to surface, but I feel nothing as I swiftly jab the needle into the back of his thigh, through the cotton of his pants and express the plunger.

Romeo jerks away like you would a painful bug bite, and the needle flies, skittering across the kitchen floor. Moaning in agony, he grasps the back of his leg as the poison spreads —burning like acid in his veins.

"Hannah." He falls into the island, barely catching himself with his hands. His eyes are glassy, his face twisted in torment as foam bubbles from his lips. He gasps once, twice, as the pulse at his throat pounds. This is how it happens. Having to battle with the digestive system, the powder is slower. It takes longer, much like swallowing a pill versus getting medicine through an IV. The liquid is quicker, much quicker, but it's not painless.

Succumbing to the fire burning through every cell in his body, Romeo crashes to his knees on the sleek tiled floor and claws at his throat before collapsing onto his side, where he contorts like a man in need of an exorcism. His mouth opens and closes like a fish, gasping for breath that doesn't come. I do nothing but stand there, inches from his feet, and watch him die. There is no comfort from me. No apologies. As kind as he was, he was complicit in the atrocities his employer enacted, and for that, I have nothing to give. No remorse. No twinge of sadness.

Eyes locked on me in fear, he reaches out with a trembling hand as if I'll comfort him.

I give him nothing.

Not a prayer.

Not even a smile.

I feel nothing as I watch life fade and his muscles cease lurching. Wide, vacant eyes stare at the ceiling as sweat trails down his forehead and foam settles like bubbles around his lips.

Romeo's death is a quick mercy, far quicker than the rest on board. That's my gift, as small as it may be.

When a sous chef races back into the kitchen and witnesses the evidence on the floor, his shrill scream echoes through the space, and still, I show no emotion. This is what I was taught. If you choose to take a life, you accept it, you own it. There is no looking back, there is no what-if, there is no sorrow. You are forever branded a killer, and that I can live with, in this moment and the hundreds of moments before. I can live with knowing these men, these scum, will never walk the face of the earth again. I did that... I freed these women. I gave them a chance at a real life, and I could never be sorry for that.

Once more, I feel nothing more than a niggle of triumph as I plunge the second needle into the shoulder of the sous chef, on his knees, trying to perform CPR on Romeo. Then, I walk away. I don't wait for him to die. I enter the dining hall, where the floor is littered with male corpses, including

Romeo's plaything, and search for the one male who had better be breathing.

Helping the group of frantic women calm down, Dark corrals them to the far side of the dining room, away from the death, and makes them sit in the same chairs the men bought them from.

When he sees me, Dark swoops in for a giant hug, pulling me right off my feet. "Thank fuck you're okay." He squeezes me fiercely and kisses one of the many hickeys he bestowed upon my flesh.

Wrapping my arms around his thick neck, I half giggle at the ridiculousness of his excitement. "I'm fine."

My ex pulls back enough to assess I'm not lying as he suspends me in the air like I weigh nothing. "You need to wash your face." He frowns, eyeing the cut and crusty nose. I can only imagine how crappy I look, but it worked, didn't it?

"It's fine." I tickle the soft hairs at the base of his head.

"No. There's still too much blood."

Ignoring his concern, I ask, "What's next?"

Grumbling at my brush-off, Dark lowers me to the ground, dragging my body down his front until I'm back on two feet. He cups the side of my face, careful not to touch the slight injury. "The brothers are hooking up now. As soon as they started dropping," he motions to the corpses, "I sent the signal."

As if on cue, men clad in all black enter the dining room, laden with duffle bags of clothes for the women, as…

"Sunshine?!" I screech when that gray-haired, bearded man comes into view, wearing the biggest damn smile.

Waiting in the middle of the space between the entrance and Dark, Sunshine puts his arms out, and I run to him, jump, and wrap my legs around his waist. He catches me with an audible "Oof" but bears the brunt of my delight as his hands get a solid hold on my ass cheeks.

"Hey, Sweets," he greets, all smiles.

"I didn't think you were coming." I play slap his shoulder in reprimand for not telling me. It wouldn't have been hard to drop a line.

Sunshine clucks his tongue. "You know me better than that. Since when have I missed cleaning up your jobs?"

"Hmmm." I think on it a beat, trying to recall a time he wouldn't have been there. When I come up short, my face scrunches in surprised disbelief. "Huh. I guess you haven't."

"Exactly. You make the messes, I clean 'em up." He winks and squeezes my cheeks to cement his point.

I tug on the tip of his beard. "That's true. But you don't have any bodies to wrap up." Usually, when he cleans, it entails his van, a couple brothers, plastic, sometimes bleach, and, occasionally, a well-thought-out fire. I poison, and they come in and clean up after me like maids but for dead bodies. They are cleaners, after all. They not only clean up my messes, but they clean up any messes the Sacred Sinners need. That's why Sunshine's a nomad. Patching into a chapter would mean roots. You can't put down deep enough roots if you're busy traveling all over the country, disposing of corpses in whatever creative means necessary.

Oh, I'm sure you're wondering why he does it and how he got into the job in the first place. It's not like someone is filling out job applications for an occupation like this. The biggest question of them all is how does he dispose of the bodies? Well, sorry to tell you, but you'll have to keep wondering because I don't even know the full backstory, and I won't ask what he does with my kills. In my mind, there's a vat somewhere where he dumps the remains, and they liquefy after a month. I think I saw something like that online when my morbid curiosity piqued. Then again, he could know someone who owns a crematorium and go that route, burning the bodies. That's probably a smarter scenario, or he could use the old-fashioned method and bury them somewhere nobody could find them. Perhaps it's a bit of both. Your guess is as good as mine.

"No," Sunshine remarks, pulling me back into the present. "But we have a boat to sink." Much like his son, Sunshine slides me down his front and resets me on my feet, but he doesn't let me go far as he grips my chin and turns my face up to get a good look at me. "Don't like seein' blood on you. You cut your face." He thumbs the underside of the wound, and I pull away, not wanting it to ache any more than it already does.

"Babe, Pops has work to do. Let's get these women on the boat," Dark calls.

"He's right," Sunshine replies. "We can catch up when I'm through." Pecking my forehead, his lips linger for half a beat before he steers me toward his son.

Needing to be helpful, I hand basic sweatshirts, sweatpants, and rubber prison-style slides to the women. They'll have better clothes when they're taken to their safe house. The Sacred Sinners have them scattered all over the country. Seemingly regular people who own regular houses in regular neighborhoods house the rescues and bikers alike until they can get them into an S.S.-affiliated rehabilitation center for trafficked women, like the place most of my sisters hail from.

Two smaller boats wait for the rescues at the stern of the yacht, at the swimming platform. I lead the women down the steps, and Dark brings up the rear. Once we reach the bottom, I step to the side as men from the boats offer their hands to help the women aboard to charter them to their larger vessel floating nearby.

"Is that for everyone?" I ask Dark, making a visor with my hand and squinting to see the boat off in the distance.

"No. They'll leave as soon as they get all the women on board. Our ride is there." Dark taps my shoulder and points in the opposite direction to a white fishing boat rocking in the water.

Nodding my understanding, I turn to address the men loading the second boat as the first speeds away. "Take good care of them," I order a burly man with face tattoos and gnarled scars slashed across his cheeks.

He snickers, and Dark pulls me to his side. "They've got this, babe."

"They'd better," I announce loud enough for everyone to hear.

With his palm held out to help another woman aboard, the scarred man snickers again. "You and Sunshine have got your hands full with that one," he comments, and I glower at him for such a ridiculous remark.

Squeezing my side in reassurance, Dark joins his brother in an unspoken manly chuckle, as if he agrees with him but won't say aloud out of fear for his life.

Ugh.

Men.

No. Not men.

Bikers.

On the boat's swimming platform, where shallow waves lick the edge, Dark and I watch the women loaded into the far-off vessel. Once they speed away, our fishing boat deploys a yellow inflatable that putters across the water faster than I expect. The single biker onboard tosses Dark the tether, and he ties it to a cleat on the yacht.

"Coal," Dark greets, clasping his brother's hand and pulling him from a boat that could be taken down with a prick of a needle. That's not reassuring, but I take it in stride as Coal, Pixie's brother, and Dark fall into easy conversation and climb the stairs back to the main part of the yacht, leaving me to bring up the rear. And boy, as much as I shouldn't, I watch them go, their butts shifting and doing all the sexy things hot men with nice asses can do in fitted bottoms. Not that I would ever say that aloud, and neither should you. This is our secret.

To bide my time before we escape this lap of luxury, I leave the men to do whatever they gotta do and lounge by the saltwater pool, soaking up the rays in my blood-speckled dress and flats. My job is done. There's nothing I can do here besides get in the way. So, I soak up the life of a rich man, imagining what it must be like to live as they do until I grow thirsty, and pour myself a glass of red at the outdoor bar before retaking the padded lounger, a hop, skip, and a jump away from the spot Dark fingered me yesterday. Man, that feels like ages ago now. Time has a way of going both slow and fast when working a job. Days drag on while moments, like yesterday, speed by, giving you whiplash in the process.

It doesn't take long for me to empty my bottle of red as my mind drifts to life and how much I'll be deconstructing the past few days for months to come.

I had sex with Dark—my ex.

Good sex.

No, incredible sex.

He cheated on his woman with me, and that didn't seem to faze him a bit.

Given our circumstances, it might have been necessary, but what if it wasn't?

What if, when he cheated on me with Abby, it didn't faze him either?

My stomach sours at the thought.

What would our sons think if they knew?

What will Sunshine think?

Did he know this would happen? And if so, why didn't he warn me?

Lost in ponderous thought, I sip the last drops of wine and stare into the pool's shimmery blue water.

Dark and I need to talk…

I have so many questions…

And I know I won't like the answers.

SIXTEEN

Sharing a fishing boat with ten celebratory men isn't what I signed up for. There is no place to escape as we ride back to shore. I'm stuck in a booth between Dark and Sunshine as other bikers fill in the gaps, locking me in the corner as they count stacks of cash on the table and drink their fill of beer. Apparently, all those rich assholes brought cash to be stored in a vault to buy the women. Now that money is S.S. property.

Less than an hour ago, we watched from our deck as the yacht and all the bodies in it went up in flames. It's now dark outside. Wind and waves knock the hull of the boat. The men don't seem to mind, but they're too busy drooling over bills to notice the mild storm brewing.

Dark slides two stacks of cash in front of me. "Yours," he announces, and the men cheer, lifting their beers, as if I'm some hero getting paid for a job well done. Not knowing what to say, I tight-lip smile in thanks.

The Sacred Sinners have always taken good care of me, not only through Dark and Sunshine but also from the higher-ups for my assistance with the sisters and my expertise, if you can even call it that. My businesses keep themselves afloat, but it wasn't always that way.

Sure, money is great, but pride and satisfaction are far greater.

When Dark notices I won't touch the cash, he tucks it into a bag I presume he's keeping for himself. There's more money there than I know what to do with. It'll likely pay off the house and then some. Like the rest of the world, that's one bill I'd like to never have to deal with again. I guess I should be grateful, but more than anything, I'm exhausted. Fighting, killing, sunbathing, and a bottle of wine takes a lot out of a lady.

Knowing I can't get out of this booth, even if I need to, I rest my head on Sunshine's shoulder and close my eyes. His hand lies on my knee under the table and remains there, heat seeping through my bare skin, as the storm outside rocks me to sleep.

SEVENTEEN

"Shhhh," a deep timbre hisses as my lids flutter open for a moment before slamming shut.

When my eyes open again, I'm moving with my head tucked against a muscled shoulder. A scruffy jaw that I'd know anywhere is the first sign Dark is carrying me. His familiar scent of bergamot, lavender, and man curls into my nose, setting me at ease when it should do anything but.

"I've got you, babe," he whispers as his boot heels scrape across the ground in a steady rhythm that lulls me back to Lala land.

When I awake again, we're no longer moving, but I'm curled in a lap with arms wrapped around me in a protective cocoon. I nuzzle my nose to the side of a throat, not of my ex's but Sunshine's. A soothing rumble percolates there as I inhale a lungful of comfort, of safety, of home, of him.

"Go back to sleep, Sweets. I've got you." Sunshine rocks me and hums a song to lull me back to dreamland.

Toying with the front of his cotton t-shirt and rolling it

between my fingers, I yawn and rub the crusties from my eyes with my fist. "I can't sleep anymore."

A small chuckle rings through the space, not from Sunshine but Dark. "Babe, we're in a hotel room for the night if you wanna sleep on a bed."

The comfy body holding me hostage snuggles me tighter. "She's fine right here." He kisses the top of my head.

"Just put her on the bed. She'll sleep better there."

Sunshine grumbles as if he doesn't like the idea, then sighs once he realizes me sleeping on something I can stretch out on is better than me curled in his lap. Either place is fine, as long as he's sleeping with me, not Dark. I can't do that again.

"How long have I been out?" I whisper to Sunshine.

"Six hours or so."

"Oh." That's longer than I thought. Then again, the boat ride took a while. But I don't remember getting off the sea, much less here. Weird.

Sunshine kisses my hair again. "Sleep all you need. We're not goin' home 'til you're rested up."

"How are we gettin' home?"

"Driving."

I nod. "Thought so." That'd been the plan since the beginning, though the details were murky. The less of a digital trail, like flight logs, the better. We don't need any of Remy's men sniffing around and pinning this on the club. After everything that popped off at the Mother Chapter, the clubhouses are already on lockdown.

"But I'll drive," Sunshine adds. "And you can play with the radio."

So, exactly what we do whenever we're in the car together. Not that I don't consider his tastes. Our music, our movies, and most things we like are similar. They always have been, except beer. Beer is vile.

"Then you need sleep, too." I poke him in the stomach.

Getting from California to home is a three-day trip unless he plans to drive a day and a half without stopping.

"I'm good, Sweets. Just need to get ya home."

This man is far too sweet for his own good. He calls me sweets when he's the sweet one. Maybe I should be the one calling him that.

Not moving from my cozy spot, I address Dark. "What are you doing?"

"Going home with you."

Right. So I won't get all the radio play time unless Sunshine forces him to sit in the back seat. Sticking Dark in the back of a car, where his legs are cramped, for days on end isn't… polite. Then again, neither is lying, cheating, or all the other shit he does. He can suffer with leg cramps. See if I care. Well, I do. Because I'm an idiot. But I'll pretend not to.

"You don't need to tidy up any Maxim Drake loose ends?" Keeping my hands busy, I lift the hem of Sunshine's shirt to touch his stomach. Just a sliver. Nothing inappropriate.

He shivers.

"No. I need to get my wife home," Dark replies.

Doing my best not to roll my eyes, even though he couldn't see them if I did, I heave a sigh. When will this man stop with the wife stuff? That part of us isn't real anymore. It's a label. One I've repeatedly asked him to stop using. Yet here we are, in a hotel room, God knows where, and I'm having to hear it all over again.

Twisting in Sunshine's embrace, I swing my legs off his

lap and set my feet on the floor. My butt nestles against his lower part, but I don't bother moving as I stare at Dark across the room, where he lounges on the other bed, his back against the old wooden headboard, ankles crossed, wearing nothing but a pair of boxer shorts. No shirt. Nothing more than muscles, ink, and our wedding band on his finger, where it doesn't belong. His hair's wet as if he just showered.

Those gray eyes bore into me from across the space.

I open my mouth to comment on the wife part, but that's not what comes out. "Did you feel bad when you cheated on me with Abby?" I ask instead, shocking the hell out of us both, and also Sunshine if his body stiffening beneath me is any indication.

"What?" Dark's jaw all but falls into his lap.

"You heard me." I didn't stutter.

"Kali." He crosses his arms beneath his pecs.

"Answer the question, Dark."

"Abby was a…" Dark drags a palm down his face and expels a pained groan as if he'd rather die than answer the question. "Listen…"

"I am listening. You're stalling."

"Why the question?" he volleys, half smug, half about to shit his pants.

Why the stalling? I want to retort but think of a better response instead. "Because you fucked me and stuck your dick in my mouth this week, and you didn't seem to care you were cheating on your woman with your ex. That's why I want to know."

Sunshine wraps his arms protectively around my middle, but I'm undeterred. Before anything else, I need to know. We can't move on from this. *I* can't move on from this without the truth. The real truth. Not some fabricated bullshit I've been fed for fucking years.

"Kali." My ex's eyes squeeze shut as if he's in physical pain. The gall of this man. Him in pain. He cheated on us both—me and Abby. He doesn't get to be in pain.

"Answer the question," I snip.

"Abby was a job, okay?" He throws his hands into the air with far more dramatics than necessary, then re-tucks them beneath his pecs and *harrumphs* as if I'm the asshole for asking.

"What do you mean, Abby was a job?" I press.

"You know how we had to have sex for this job?"

"Yesss." My eyes widen in horror as a light bulb clicks on in my head. "Abby was a… job. Oh. Ohhhh." He was assigned to her. To fuck her. To do whatever… ick. Just… ick.

Dark stares at the wall, refusing to look directly at me. "I was ordered to do some shit I can't tell you about. She was part of it."

"For how long?"

"Months."

This piece of shit.

"You fucked her for months?" I seethe. Months. Not days. Not weeks. Months.

My ex nods twice. "It was part of the job, so yes."

"Was getting her pregnant part of the job?" I sass back.

"No." He scowls like I've somehow offended him. "Of course not. That was an accident. That's the only reason I didn't come home sooner."

Hold up.

Am I hearing this right?

Are you hearing this right?

Did he say what I think he just said?

"You fucked this woman for months, and had she *not* gotten pregnant, you would have come home sooner?!" I shrill and try to stand, but Sunshine's there, forcing me to remain on his lap with his iron grip digging into my hips so I can't launch myself across the room and punch my ex-husband in the jaw or, worse, castrate him with a knife. His knife. I'm sure he has one in his bag. I'll put them in a jar on my nightstand as a morbid trophy. Or maybe I'll bury them in my garden. They'll make the perfect fertilizer. Hell, let's bury him in the garden. Daisies will look extra pretty, blooming out of his eye sockets.

Closing his eyes, Dark shakes his head. "Of course, I would have come home sooner. You're my wife. I wanted to be with my wife. I didn't want to be there. But that's what I was ordered to do."

Oh, poor Dark, forced to screw a sexy, younger woman for months. Please excuse me while I weep for him.

"Hold up." I lift my hand to collect my thoughts and temper my growing anger. I blow out a breath, then another, before I speak again. "You would have come home and never told me about Abby had she not gotten pregnant? You cheated on me, and you weren't going to tell me?"

Looking up to the ceiling, yellowed from years of smoke, Dark massages the nape of his neck and rolls his shoulders. My jailer removes his hold on my hips as we wait a solid minute for his son to answer. "Kali. Babe. It…It's not like that," he tries and fails to sound convincing.

Refusing to back down, I dig a little deeper. "You stuck your dick, the one I was married to, into another pussy that didn't belong to me, and you weren't going to tell me you cheated. How many times did this happen, Dark?"

My ex's throat rolls as he swallows thickly. "Kali. Please. Don't." His voice is hoarse. But it's not good enough. I need to know.

"Answer the goddamn question." Foot bouncing, my anger's replaced with anxiety. Because this is it. He's gonna tell me. Finally, after all these years, he's being honest not only with me but himself.

His nostrils flare. "No."

"Why?" I push, knowing I've got him right where I want him. There's no getting out of this now. He has no place to go. No place to hide. "Because it was more than Abby, wasn't it? You cheated on me multiple times, didn't you? And you felt nothing when you cheated on Abby with me because… because you… oh, my, Mother Earth, you do it to her, too, don't you?"

Dropping his gaze, Dark stares straight ahead at the ugly, yellow flower wallpaper. Tears trickle down his cheeks, and his bottom lips wobble as if talking about his cheating ways is ripping him apart. Fuck that. He did this. He doesn't get to be sad about it.

When Dark doesn't reply, I keep going, and Sunshine's arms curl around me in a band of comfort and support. "How many women did you cheat on me with?"

"None."

"Liar!" I snarl.

My ex swipes the wetness from his face with the back of his hand. "I have no love for anyone I've ever slept with, Kali, except you. It doesn't matter how many pussies I've fucked. It doesn't matter why I had to fuck them. I have never loved a single person as much as I love you. You are my wife. That's what I keep fuckin' telling you. That's why I won't divorce you. You. Are. My. Wife!" Dark roars, punching the air. Face flushed, the muscles in his neck and chest tighten as he slams his fist into the bed, growling like a caged beast. Throwing his skull into the headboard, it ricochets off the wall as he beats the mattress on either side of him again and again until the veins in his forearms pop.

Swallowing down the lump in my throat, I whisper, "I hate you."

How could someone do the things he has?

I poison people and feel nothing. But even I would never consider hurting the one I claim to love. Not for anything in the world.

"Christ, I know! I live with that every fuckin' goddamn day."

"And now you're hurting Abby," I shoot back. Sunshine rubs my stomach as if trying to calm me.

Twisting to look at me straight-on, Dark shows zero remorse when he states, "I don't care about Abby."

Bile rises in my throat at his conviction. That's the mother of his child. She deserves more than this. "That's horrible! Don't say that. Take it back."

"No. I won't. She's nice. I like her fine enough. But I don't love her. You don't just love someone because you have sex with 'em. You can't fall in love with someone else if you're already in love. It doesn't work like that. Ask Pops why he doesn't have a woman, Kali. Ask him why he doesn't date." Dark lifts his chin at his father, goading him to say something.

"Dark," Sunshine rumbles in warning.

Peeling the older biker's arms from around my waist, I pad to the front of the room to get a little space. Shaking my arms down at my sides, I pace the distance between the front door and the ancient television on the even older dresser. It's missing a drawer. Literal cobwebs fill the dark space. There are only a few feet to move about, but it helps me focus. I shouldn't have asked Dark. I don't even want to know all this, but I need to know. I need… to be freed.

Ignoring Dark for a moment, I face Sunshine. "Did you know about Abby? Did you know what Dark does?" I gesture between the two of them.

Much like his son, Sunshine drags a palm down his face. That simple motion confirms my worst fears.

He. Knew.

"You lied to me," I croak. "You said you didn't know where Dark was."

Sitting on the edge of the bed, Sunshine rubs his knees. "I know."

A lone tear breaks free and slides down my cheek to the tip of my chin, where it falls to the ground.

"You knew about the cheating." My voice wobbles.

A shallow, solemn nod is his only reply.

Fuck.

Just like that, my entire world implodes. Rushing to the bathroom, I slam the door shut, lock it, and press my back against the cool wood as I shatter. Ugly sobs rack my body as I slide to the floor, and pain unlike I've ever experienced before rips from the depths of my already fucked-up soul.

I trusted them.

The men I loved most in the world.

The men who saved me from a lonely life.

Everything has been a lie.

Our marriage.

The friendship.

Dark and Sunshine frantically pound on the door. The force rattles through my spine as snot runs down my face.

Knees pulled to my chest, I rest my chin there and cry, and cry until I can cry no more. Until every broken piece of me lay at my feet—shards of glass tinged with blood. My blood. From trusting them. From… my stupidity.

"Kali!" Dark roars. "I'm sorry." He beats his fist against the doorframe. "I'm so fuckin' sorry, babe."

But he's not.

He did this.

He made his choices.

And his father went along with it.

They're no better than the men I kill.

No. They're worse.

I trusted them.

"I never want to… to see you again!" Rubbing my salty anguish into either shoulder of my dress, I draw shaky circles across my shins. "Never, ever, ever, ever, again," I announce quieter.

"Sweets, please, let's talk about it," Sunshine reasons, tone scratchy as if he, too, is crying.

But I don't reply.

Because they win.

They ruined everything.

I have nothing left to give.

They lied.

They broke me.

It's over.

The End

For Now…

Printed in Great Britain
by Amazon

55021191R00117